Finding Erin

Evangeline Duran Fuentes

This is a work of fiction. Names, characters,
businesses, places, events and incidents are
either the products of the author's imagination
or used in a fictitious manner. Any resemblance to
actual persons, living or dead, or actual events is
purely coincidental.

Pipe & Thimble Publishing
Lomita, CA

Printed in the United States of America
10 9 8 7 6 5 4 3 2 1

ISBN-13: 978-0692196250
ISBN-10: 0692196250

With much love and appreciation, I dedicate the humble writings of this story to my dearest friend, Dr. Sonia Ceballos. For without her skills, knowledge, determination and stamina, I would not have been here to create and complete this endeavor. I love and thank you with this simple heart that you saved, so many years ago.

*Forever in your debt,
Ms. Fuentes*

Acknowledgments

This story was written to entertain as well as give insight to the challenges and heartfelt experiences that are a result of memory loss.

I give my warmest thanks to my family, both by DNA and of the heart, for their infinite patience, their loving smiles, and their tears while helping me cross the bridge from nothingness to everything possible.

To my dearest friend and publisher, Barb Lieberman, who continues to believe in me. And, with every word and action, helps me to achieve my dream.

To my dear friend, author, editor and most efficient P.A., Ellie Lieberman, for all she does behind the scenes to make me look brilliant.

To Toni Kerr of TKArtistry for her incredible skill and talent in designing my cover. Who listened to my ideas and created a reality.

To the incredible Ferris Molina, editor extraordinaire, for his patience and skill in taking my rough manuscript and making it readable.

And last, to my amazing husband for his patience and good humor. Most importantly, for his support, encouragement and belief in my ability to tell a story, put it on paper and share it with the world.

My heart fills with love and gratitude for all the kindness.

Foreword

Her face looked dusky. A color I knew all too well from my previous experience working as an Emergency room nurse. I called out her name with no response. I dropped the wound change supplies and ran to her bedside. I placed my fingers on her carotid and my cheek above her mouth and nose. No pulse. No chest rise and fall. No breath against my cheek.

"Code blue, Code blue!" I ripped the resuscitative air support bag that hangs from each hospital bed and jumped on her bed to begin chest compressions while providing oxygen through the "ambu bag." The code team arrived, and leads were placed on her chest. There was no cardiac activity except that of my chest compressions. The "code" continued as I refused to give up my position and stop chest compressions. This was *my* patient. I wasn't giving up on her.

It was the morning of November 23, 2006. And, though it was Thanksgiving Day, it was the same as every other morning since the day I began my intern year of residency in Obstetrics and Gynecology four months earlier. It is the job of the intern to take care of the "To Do" list on all patients admitted to our service. So, after morning rounds with our chief residents and attending, we all settled into our tasks for the day. Behind the scenes, the nurses were preparing a Thanksgiving feast which helped offset the sobering fact that we had to spend the holiday away from our families. (Not to mention being able to escape hospital cafeteria food for a day! Truly, something to be thankful for!)

While waiting for the elevator, on my way to complete my last task of the morning, one of the nurses called out to me, "Come have Thanksgiving lunch!" It was tempting. I was hungry. And, my "Wound Change" wasn't going anywhere. Still, I thought it would be better to enjoy lunch with a completed "To Do" list. So, I turned and responded with, "I have one more thing to do and then I'll head right up." I'd inherited this patient from another service for the holiday. We'd never met, but the words of my mentor during medical school and subsequent attending physician at Harbor UCLA were forever etched into my mind: "Sonia, every patient is your grandmother, mother, sister, or 'tia.' Treat her the way you would want your family to be treated."

I continued chest compressions looking up only once during the code to find my chief resident and attending staring at me in bewilderment from the hospital room doorway. It was clear they had forgotten, or perhaps had never known two things: First, I was an E.R. nurse before I was a doctor. I may have been a new intern, but I was not new to medical emergencies.

Second, I chose to attend the medical school that brought me to this very day because of its commitment to educational excellence (UCLA) *and* to the underserved (Charles R. Drew University). In our class of 175 at the UCLA School of Medicine, I was one of 24 students who had made the commitment to serve the underserved throughout our careers as physicians. Harbor-UCLA, located in the heart of one of the most underserved communities in Los Angeles, was the perfect place for me. I was in love with the community—with *"mi gente"*—and I was *not giving up on this patient!*

"We got her back!" the physician running the code shouted. I jumped off the side of her bed. My arms were trembling, and my body and brow were dripping in sweat. I was relieved. Happy. And quietly rejoicing. This is how I met Mrs. Evangeline Fuentes.

The following morning, I headed home for the remainder of the holiday weekend. On Monday, I went to see how she was doing. *My God she's awake!* was my first thought as I walked in to find a perky and talkative Mrs. Fuentes. I introduced myself and she said, "I'm not remembering anything. How do I know you?" I don't know what I said, but I remember thinking, *Oh, shit, she doesn't remember anything!*

For the next three and a half years of my residency, I saw Mrs. Fuentes and her husband, Ray, on most holidays when they'd stop by the hospital to drop off a delicious meal or treat. And, there were other occasions, outside of work, when we'd meet to share a cup of coffee, a cerveza, or a bowl of menudo. To this day, the tradition continues. And, with each new visit, we find another detail one of us is unaware of regarding that fateful day.

She has become a friend and a confidant. She

has shared in some of my dearest and most personal life events even though hundreds of miles now separate us. She is the heart emoji I can count on with every picture or story I post about my children on Facebook. She is one of the coolest, kindest, and most compassionate people I know. I thank God, I had to work on that Thanksgiving Day so many years ago. The world needs Mrs. Evangeline Fuentes. We're all better off because of the way she lives and loves.

It was an honor to be asked to be a part of this book—*her* book. I celebrate the life of "Angie" before and after November 23, 2006. May you all enjoy reading about this relatable and wonderful, "Home girl" whose passion for life and living has brought her this far.

Sonia Ceballos, MD, FACOG

Jim

Jim hadn't been home for more than a few minutes when the phone rang.

"Mr. Berger, this is Dr. Chan. I'm one of Erin's doctors. I don't mean to scare you, but there really isn't any easy way to say this. Your wife, Erin... was found non-responsive. They're working on her as we speak. You need to get back to the hospital as soon as possible."

"What? What is that, non-responsive? What are you talking about?" Immediately, Jim's heart thumped, closing up his throat as a cold chill scrambled up his spine.

Dr. Chan cleared his throat.

"Her heart stopped, and she stopped breathing. As of this moment, her body is still not responding. The Cardiac Team will continue to try and resuscitate her. But, we can't be sure of the outcome."

"No! You're mistaken, Dr. Chan!" Jim argued. "Did you, yourself, personally examine her? She's just tired; she's sleeping. I just left her not more than fifteen minutes ago, and she said she was going to take a nap, but she was fine." Jim laughed, nervously. "It can't be, Dr. Chan."

"I'm sorry, Mr. Berger. There is no mistake. I suggest you come back to the hospital immediately, sir."

"I'm on my way." Jim murmured, his voice just above a whisper.   At that very moment, he didn't recognize the trembling sound of his own words. He grabbed his jacket and, as he ran out the door, he shouted out to his daughter, "Something's wrong with your mom. I'll call you later."

He was only five minutes away, yet it seemed to take an eternity to get to the hospital. During the short drive, all Jim kept saying to himself was, "They're wrong, she's fine! She's just a little tired." Then in a crazed rage, "They don't know what the hell they're talking about. They're crazy or stupid. I don't know which, but I know there's a mistake somewhere. Hell, it's a teaching hospital, so what the heck do they know? They're all just learning. God, please let Dr. Chan be wrong! Please!"

Praying was not something Jim did on a daily basis, and, at the moment, he didn't consider that he was saying a prayer. He was just talking out loud to whomever or whatever was out there in the Universe, listening.

Jim caught every red light and, when he finally reached the hospital, finding a parking space became the real challenge. He grumbled to himself and ultimately cursed everything and everyone in his sight. Angry, worried, and confused, he stalked the parking lot, finally lucking out. A little old lady was pulling out of a spot, so he leaned out of the window and barked at her to hurry up and get out of the way. She had barely cleared the parking space when pulled in with a screech.

Finally parked, he ran out of the car, forgetting and not caring to lock the car door, rushing through the hospital doors, only to get stuck in front of the elevator, waiting. After an exasperating few minutes, his mind pondering all the possibilities and his heart aching to hear Erin's voice, Jim finally reached the fourth floor and raced out of the elevator toward Erin's room, practically knocking over the people waiting on the other side of the door.

Jim eventually got to Erin's room, but the entrance was blocked, and he couldn't get in. He stood trapped in the open doorway, unable to cross the threshold. A multitude of onlookers were backed up to the door, while doctors, nurses, and technicians were around the bed, all feverishly working on someone.

Orders were barked, and responses were shouted in return. Someone was starting an I.V. in the patient's arm, and several plastic pouches of liquid were being hung on the I.V. pole. The hissing sound of the blood pressure cuff being inflated and slowly deflated could be faintly heard, secondary to all the commotion.

"It can't be Erin," he thought.

He heard someone yell, "Clear!" and the mass of people took a step back. Then, he heard the loud *ZAP!* and, at that moment, he felt like he had been hit in the back of his knees. His legs weakened, wanting to go out from under him. Jim held onto the door jamb for support and the reality of the situation hit him, *hard*! It *was* Erin they were working on!

Jim wanted to yell, "Erin, I'm right here." But, all that came out was a low whimper. His throat was tight, like a tie strangling his Adam's apple and cutting off his oxygen supply. His stomach turned upside down, then tightened like a vice-grip pinching his lower abdomen.

Jim looked up through the sea of employees and caught a glimpse of a small woman, perched, kneeling on top of the bed, shouting out orders. Her slender arms were locked in a stiff position, and it appeared she was vigorously pushing on the patient's chest. The sight of the proceedings weakened Jim's stamina, pushing him into a daze. Lightheaded, Jim held tight to the wall to maintain his footing.

"Mr. Berger? Are you okay?" An arm slid across Jim's shoulders to steady his balance. It was Dr. Chan. "Get a chair," he ordered, and an employee quickly slipped a chair under Jim.

"Erin?" was all that Jim could whisper.

"We're doing everything possible," Dr. Chan explained. "We just have to wait and see. Don't give up hope."

Erin Berger had recently undergone abdominal surgery to remove what she thought was a small, insignificant speck on her left ovary. Instead, what started out as a tiny lesion seven months earlier, had grown to over three-and-a-half inches in size and attached itself to her intestines. The surgery, that should have only taken approximately half an hour, took the surgeons over four hours to remove all of the webbed tendrils that encased and attached the tumor to Erin's intestines. This was to be a simple procedure compared to the open-heart surgery she had undergone in March of that same year.

Immediately after Erin's triple bypass, a routine CT scan was performed to make sure her heart was working properly, and it was. But, that was when the minuscule lesion was detected. By the time an Ultrasound and surgery could be scheduled, it was late October, and that's when Erin's life took a rough turn.

The operation to remove the lesion was successful, and four days later, after happily receiving the report that there were no traces of cancer, she was discharged and sent home to recuperate.

The uneventful week passed quickly and, six days after her discharge, Erin made the trip back to the clinic for a follow-up visit to have her surgical staples removed. She was a little sore but feeling great and ready to slowly get back to all her normal activities.

Unfortunately, things didn't go quite as she had planned. Within less than an hour of arriving home from the clinic, excruciating pain gripped her lower abdomen. Bent over, clutching her stomach, she cautiously made her way to the bathroom and discovered an enormous amount of blood-like liquid oozing from her abdomen and running down her legs. Her recent surgical wound had eviscerated, opened up like a zipper being pulled apart from one hip to the other.

Immediately, she grabbed a towel and held it tight to her open wound, screaming hysterically for Jim. Within minutes of calling 911, Erin was whisked away to the Emergency Room with Jim right behind. And, once again, she became a temporary resident of the hospital.

The cause of such a bloody scare was a wound infection that had settled in her abdominal cavity, inhibiting the tissue from healing and her wound from closing. Erin was admitted to the hospital, and I.V. antibiotics and pain medication were started. Orders were written for both medications to be administered around the clock, along with dressing changes, irrigation, and packing of the wound every four hours.

The same routine, except for changes in the nursing staff, continued for two and a half weeks, with Erin and Jim becoming favorites of the nurses, technicians, and housekeeping staff.

Jim's attention to Erin, in the way of assisting with her baths and linen changes, relieved the over-worked nurses, for which they were extremely grateful.   His cheery attitude and generous nature to all the staff were welcomed.

Every few days, he brought in something for the nurses' station. Whether it was cookies or donuts or a tray of fresh fruit or vegetables, it didn't matter. All were thankfully received and definitely endeared the couple to the fourth-floor staff.

After approximately two weeks, Erin's wound appeared to be healing. But, from one day, it suddenly changed in color and gave rise to a spike in her temperature, causing her appetite to vanish along with her energy.

Against Erin's strong protests, Jim immediately decided he would stay at her side, day and night, until the fever broke. With the help of the nurses, by way of blankets and a pillow, Jim made himself a comfortable nest in a chunky, over-used chair, right next to Erin's bed.

Thanksgiving was three days away and, sadly, unless her condition changed drastically for the better, she wouldn't be home to celebrate with her family. Not that a turkey dinner was on her mind. Eating was the last thing she wanted to do. Of late, all Erin wanted to do was sleep.

So, for three days, she did just that. With Jim patiently at her side, wiping her brow and holding not only her hand, but, when needed or when she asked, her whole body.

Much to the dismay of the nursing staff, he would carefully climb into the hospital bed, alongside Erin, and wrap his arms around her, cradling and soothing her exhausted frame. Spooning, comforting, and reassuring his wife of thirty-five years, not only with words but with a soft touch, a caress, and, at times, just with his presence. Jim could calm all of Erin's fears and anxieties with gentle ease.

Magic Connection

On that particular Thanksgiving Day in 2006, Erin watched from her hospital bed as Jim's eyes lazily closed and a soft snore escaped through his nose and a short toot slipped out of his bottom. He had been by her side, hanging out in that old, lumpy chair, occasionally leaving her only to get something to eat from the vending machines in the hallway and to use the restroom.

Her condition had his nerves frazzled and his lower back muscles all twisted in a knot. His neck and shoulders appeared tight, and the spasms that made him twitch confirmed the tension that Jim kept denying. Since the doctors finally thought they had a handle on Erin's condition, and possibly had it under control, he was beginning to loosen up. Or, maybe, it was just that fatigue had finally won out and taken over, causing his heavy eyelids to slide down and shut tight.

How lucky am I, thought Erin, to h*ave someone love me so much that he gives up his comfort and sleeps all twisted up like a pretzel, just to make sure I'm okay? Here I am with no make-up, my hair in a loose bun on the top of my head and my eyes with big, dark circles under them, looking like something left over from an unsuccessful yard sale. Yet, he still looks at me as if I were a size eight, twenty-year-old beauty queen contestant.*

A tender comfort embraced her, knowing that every time she opened her eyes, it was Jim's face she would see. He would be right there, waiting for her to open hers. At the same time, she felt it was unfair to him. A tinge of guilt twisted inside her that he wasn't getting the rest or proper nourishment he deserved and needed. Jim getting run down was the last thing she wanted.

Erin loved him more than life itself. In her heart, he was, always had been, and always would be, the love of her life. His life and well- being, as well as that of her children, were Erin's number one concern. The fact that currently she wasn't able to look after and care for him like the worthy husband he was distressed her.

Approximately thirty-five years before, like a knight in shining armor, Jim had come to her rescue when she didn't even know she needed saving. It had been that way since the day she met him at a funky little church dance. He extended his open hand and softly asked, "May I have this dance, Ma'am?" The moment Erin tucked her hand in his, magic sparked. He slid his strong, muscular arm around her then-small waist and, like two pieces of a thousand-piece puzzle, they fit. Right there in the middle of the crowded dance floor, his quick wit and sense of humor swept her off her feet. The instant he opened his mouth and, in his slow Texas drawl, compared their fancy dance steps to Fred Astaire and Ginger Rogers, Erin knew he was the one. This polite, southern gentleman had lassoed, tied, and pulled her right into his life.

She had never met anyone her age interested or even familiar with the famous dance team of the Thirty's. His knowledge of the legendary duo and their movies, along with his charming good looks and the sexy way he smelled, melted her heart. From that day forward, the two were infinitely connected. Thirty-five years later, they still giggled, danced, and managed to make each other sigh, just like that first night in the church auditorium.

And, now, instead of being at home, sitting in his cushy recliner and watching TV, here he was, drained and all scrunched up in that worn-out, bumpy chair, worried sick about her.

"Honey," whispered Erin. "Go home." Talking out loud was out of the question. Not because it was a hospital but because her worn out body didn't have the energy. "You need some rest, my love. Go and get some sleep in our own bed and have a decent meal. If you don't, you'll end up here, just like me. Can you imagine both of us lying here? What a fine pair we'd make. Go! I'll be fine."

Jim stirred with the sandman's glaze still covering his eyes and a coy smile on his lips, he said, "We'd be stuck together like peanut butter and jelly, snuggling close and delicious. Besides, I wasn't sleeping. I was just giving my eyelids a little vacation. You know, just resting the old peepers."

"Well, rest them at home. Go on now," she ordered in a hushed, yet firm tone. "You'll feel so much better after you take a hot shower and get in a little snooze or maybe take a peek at your Cowboys. You know you would enjoy that."

Jim stood up and torpidly stretched. "You know, I could watch the game right here with you," he cooed.

"Oh, no you won't," Erin countered. "You get too excited and make too much noise. It is a hospital, or have you forgotten?"

Jim leaned over the hospital bed rail and whispered in Erin's ear, "Are you sure you'll be okay? I hate to leave you here all by yourself."

"I'm not all by myself," she murmured. Her voice not much above a whisper. "The nurses are here. I'm fine, truly. My fever is going down, and I'm just a little tired. Now go, get out of here for a little bit! Anyway, it's almost time for my dressing change and those super drugs they give me for the pain will put my lights out for a good while."

"I'm not too comfortable leaving you right now. You look pale and kind of worn out. You hardly have enough air to get the words out. You sure you're okay?"

"I'm fine! And, you've asked me that more times than I want to remember. Get out of here!" Erin wouldn't listen to his protests. Whatever she was feeling, she would keep to herself.

It was true, she was extremely tired, more so than she had been in the last few days. Her fever was down. Accordingly, she should be feeling a lot better. Not having enough air to speak or the strength to keep her eyes open didn't make sense. But, none of that was important at the moment. Allowing Jim to rest and have a little bit of time to himself was what mattered.

"All right! But, you gotta promise to get some sleep while I'm gone. I'll go, but just for a little while. I'm beginning to smell kind of ripe, and I know that can't be too healthy for you. Are your nose hairs singeing from my 'stank', baby?"

Erin smiled weakly, "No! But, a little soap and water *and* deodorant couldn't hurt."

"Okay! Okay! Wash, dry, and powder is first on the agenda. Maybe a little cologne to get your hormones excited," Jim teased with a wink and a smile. "I'll eat some turkey and cornbread dressing for both of us and maybe watch just enough of the Cowboys game to get the score. And, then, I'll be right back. Can I bring you back some 'tater salad? You know it's your favorite."

Erin scrunched her face and slowly shook her head "no".

"Okay? I won't be long," Jim said. "Keep smiling for me and don't miss me too much!"

Erin didn't answer, she smiled feebly and nodded. Sighing softly, she closed her eyes and, as Jim walked out of her hospital room, drifted off into a fitful slumber.

She knew, in her heart, if she asked or even looked as if she wanted him to stay, he would. But, he needed some time for himself. And, in truth, she knew he wouldn't get any sleep. The Cowboys were playing, and there was no way in Hell that Jim would miss out on watching Dallas play. Football was the only entertainment that Jim fanatically enjoyed. And, being from Texas, the Cowboys were number one.

Today, more than ever, Erin felt that Jim desperately needed a break. Just a few minutes to take his mind off her medical ordeal and to have a real home-cooked meal. With their daughter preparing the Thanksgiving feast, it was the perfect opportunity for him to eat a good meal and enjoy some of the football game without worrying that he might get loud and overly enthusiastic, causing a ruckus in her hospital room.

It was also a good time for Erin to sleep, without feeling guilty about him sitting in the chair watching her every breath and jumping up each time she moved. After everything he and Erin had been through recently, the game would be a great distraction for him.

It's how their life flowed. Erin worried about Jim, and Jim fretted over Erin. There was a magic that swirled between them and encased them in a space all their own. They finished one another's thoughts as well as their sentences. And, in a room full of people, be they friends, relatives or strangers, one look between them and no one else existed. It's just the way it was and always had been.

Code Blue

Changing Erin Berger's dressing was never an easy task. She was a fairly-thick woman, consequently, the abdominal wound was quite deep, stretching from hip to hip, and approximately six inches deep in the center. One could place an open hand in the wound, and it would almost disappear.

First and foremost, the routine was extremely agonizing for Erin. Thus, Morphine was always administered, prior to the procedure, to alleviate some of the pain. And, every four hours, without fail, the technique was performed. First, unpacking the wound and irrigating it with sterile saline and Betadine solution. Then, repacking it until the wide, gauze strips were even with the top of the skin. All steps were necessary to keep the wound clean and the infection at bay. According to the doctor, the wound needed to heal from the inside out.

Erin was told that due to her Diabetes, it would take months, but it would heal. The key was to keep her sugar down and the infection under control.

Since it was Thanksgiving Day, a potluck was underway at the nurses' station and the nurses had fixed a dinner plate of holiday delicacies for Dr. Cabral. Everyone tried to persuade her to eat first, then see to her patient. But, as usual with Sara Cabral, her patients came first.

The talk at the nurses' station was that she

was always the first intern at the hospital in the morning and the last one to leave. So committed was she to her patients, and to the oath she took to care for them, that nothing stood in the way of that devotion. She was that high-caliber of physician.

Rumor had it that she had been an E.R. nurse prior to becoming a doctor, and although she loved her work, she wanted to do more than just nurse her patients; she wanted to have more control and authority regarding their care. Being an R.N. wasn't enough, so she went back to school and became a doctor, her patients the beneficial recipients of her determination. It wasn't an easy task financially, mentally, or spiritually. But, once she had made up her mind, there was nothing to stop her. She had everything she needed: courage, perseverance and the loving support of her family and the love of her life.

As an intern at one of the largest teaching hospitals on the West Coast, she still didn't have the control she so desired. After all, she was still just a *lowly* intern, the lowest rung on the medical ladder.

Presently, her opinions, thoughts, skills and knowledge held very little value. But, every minute of her working days and nights was dedicated to the healing, comfort, and well-being of the patients in her capable hands. The respect she deserved was forthcoming and, when it was finally awarded, she would welcome it, knowing she had earned it.

Erin Berger was Dr. Sara Cabral's last patient to attend and her dressing change was the tired physician's final task of the day. "I'll just finish dressing this last patient," she thought. "Then I can take my time and enjoy my meal before I head for home."

Smiling, the young intern walked into the ward, ready to tackle the dressing change, her arms overflowing with all the supplies needed: bandages, sterile saline, a bottle of Betadine solution, gauze, gloves and a hypodermic syringe filled with Morphine, to be administered through the I.V. at the time of the procedure. She entered Erin's room, cheerfully announcing her presence.

"Lucky you, Mrs. Berger. It's that time of..." One glance at her patient at the end of the room, and her voice trailed off. Instantly, her day took on a swift change.

"*Code Blue! Code Blue, 4217B, 4217B!*" she screamed as she dropped everything and ran to the patient's side.

The patient's face a pale blue in color and wide, bulging eyes staring blankly up at the ceiling, told a frightening story. Her small hands were tightly balled up into stiff bluish-purple fists, clutching the sheet tightly up against her neck.

Dr. Cabral yanked the sheet away. Due to her petite stature, she needed to be up higher than her patient in order to have the leverage needed to perform her duties efficiently. Without even thinking, she jumped on the bed, knelt beside her patient and did what she had to do. With all her strength, she proceeded to pound the woman's chest with her closed fist, hoping to kick-start the woman's heart.

Wham! The patient's body bounced up with the tremendous force of the blow to the chest. The young physician felt Erin's neck for a pulse, then listened intently with her stethoscope, with no response. The heart refused to react. Again, she pounded on the chest with her clenched fist and listened for some sign of life.

Quickly, methodically, and efficiently, the intern began C.P.R.

Within seconds, the Cardiac Arrest Team arrived, and a medical ballet began.

Technicians, nurses, and doctors all worked together to save this woman's life. Each one performed a specific duty, independent of each other and no one got in anyone else's way. Not once did a hand, an arm, or any body part intrude in another person's work- space. And, never did the young doctor waver on her self-assigned task of saving her patient's life.

The procedure was initiated by the team immediately placing a cardiac board behind Erin's back to keep her body from sinking into the mattress while CPR was being performed. Next, an intubation tube was inserted into her mouth, through her throat, and down into her windpipe to introduce the flow of oxygen into her lungs.

Normally, protocol would have dictated that, when the Cardiac Team arrived with the Crash Cart, they'd take control of the situation, allowing the person who found the patient to catch his or her breath and rest for a moment. A rotation would begin with the doctors taking turns, one stimulating the heart and another administering forced air through the intubation tube into the patient's lungs. But, in this particular instance, Dr. Cabral refused to stop what she was doing.

"This is my patient, and I take full responsibility," she adamantly informed the team, and she continued her labors.

The paddles on the defibrillator were primed with a liquid gel, and an electrical charge was used to shock Erin Berger's heart.

"*Clear!*" someone shouted. Everyone took a step backward.

A crashing *ZAP!* was heard, and Erin's body bounced up off the bed. The deteriorating heart produced two weak beats and stopped again.

The young physician yelled, "*Again!*" And, once more, the electrical jolt resounded with such force, the lights appeared to dim, if for only a second. The life-saving dance continued.

Twice, through the harrowing Cardiac Arrest, Dr. Cabral's chief resident physician, Dr. Chan, tugged at her sleeve and said," She's gone, Sara. You've done all you can do. Let her go!" The intern didn't look up or slow her actions.

"No! Not on my watch! She *will* respond, I know it!" With that said, she bellowed out orders for more medication to be administered through the I.V. Dr. Cabral felt it in her heart and, just like her stubbornness demanded, Erin Berger's heart eventually began a weak, yet steady rhythm, much to everyone's surprise and elation, causing embarrassment to more than just a few.

It took a total of twenty-three minutes of constant manipulation of Erin Berger's heart and lungs for Dr. Cabral to stabilize the heart sufficiently to transport Erin up to the Intensive Care Unit.

The young healer never left her side. She remained perched on top of the bed, kneeling alongside her patient and continued to push air with the Am-bu bag into Erin's weak lungs.

Following her cardiac ordeal, Erin Berger lapsed into a coma and remained there for approximately three days ...

Her family, her husband in particular, eyes swimming in tears, the soles of his shoes worn from pacing the halls, pleaded with whomever in the Universe was listening. Their outlook on Erin's future was as dim and dreary as the rain-filled clouds that shrouded the Southern California sky. The doctor remained hopeful but unsure.

"Until she wakes, we can't make a concrete prognosis as to her outcome." Dr. Chan's eyes looked up to face Jim Berger. "As you know, we have no idea how long she was lying there without circulation to her system.

"Dr. Cabral reported that when she walked into the room, Erin was completely non-responsive, her face and hands were blue and her body, cold and stiff. It could have been maybe six or eight minutes, perhaps even longer without circulation and definitely without oxygen to the brain.

"If she comes through this, she could have substantial brain damage. She could be partially or completely paralyzed, blind, mute or deaf, and her memory could be totally erased. You need to be prepared for the worst. It is possible for Erin to never come out of the coma. At this point in time, difficult as it is, I want you to understand the full complexity of the situation and the severity."

Dr. Chan shook Jim's hand. Then, without explanation, he reached up and hugged the large, shattered man. He turned and slowly walked out of the door. His slumped shoulders, lowered eyes and head, told the story of a doctor with no solid answers and no comfort for a grieving family.

Jim sat in a chair on the side of the bed holding Erin's hand up to his lips, gently kissing her fingertips. "Come on, Angel! Open your eyes. Tell me to shut up or get out of here, anything! Just open your eyes. I know you can hear me, Erin. I know you can. Please, baby. Let me know you're okay." The tears flooded his eyes, spilled out, trailed down his cheeks and slowly slid onto his bushy mustache.

How could something like this happen? he wondered. One minute he was there at her side, laughing and joking, and she was fine. Okay, she was tired, and she didn't want to eat, but that was nothing new. She had been feeling like that for a few days.

The doctors thought it was because of the infection, and they said it wasn't uncommon. Now, they were saying she might not come out of this. And, if she did, she might be a vegetable.

"I'll need to have a ramp installed in the front of the house. Changes will have to be made to accommodate a wheelchair or a hospital bed." Jim's thoughts were reeling and jumping from one thing to another. "What if she can't remember me? Or the kids? What then? Her whole life might be over. Our life, as we know it, will be over."

It had been three days and not even a twitch was detected in Erin's face. Nothing! Not a single bit of progress was visible. Jim sat by her side and continued to question the reasons for Erin's condition. What could have caused her heart to just stop? Was she so tired that she just gave up on life?

"Please, Erin! Give me a sign. Squeeze my hand, open your eyes, tell me to go to hell if you want! Say anything! Please, baby. I'm right here!"

The comatose patient heard every word of his aching plea. But, hard as she tried, she couldn't move. Who was this person asking, and even demanding, for someone to do something? It sounded like a desperate man, but who was he? And, who was this Erin person that he kept talking to?

Why couldn't she open her eyes?

"I'm tired, please go away and let me sleep." Fuzzy thoughts and confusion swirled in her mind. She had a lot of questions but, at the moment, exhaustion and pain controlled her whole body. All she wanted to do was sleep.

A New Day

"Good morning, Erin! Take a deep breath and open up those pretty eyes of yours! Come on, now. Take a deep breath and open up your eyes. You can do it! I know you can. Erin! Open your eyes and take a deep breath."

Choking on the tube in her throat, Erin frantically tried to speak but only gagged.

"I can't take that tube out of your mouth until I know you can breathe on your own. So, take a deep breath!" said the nurse, firm in her instructions to Erin.

"Who is that? And why is she yelling?" Erin took a deep breath.

"That's right, I know you can hear me. Now, Erin, open your eyes!"

"Who the hell is Erin? I know she's not talking to me! My name is…? Oh God! What is my name? I can't remember!" She tried to reach her hand out but couldn't. Her hands were tied down. Instantly, Erin's claustrophobia fiercely kicked in and her eyes flew open. A gravely groan from deep in her chest came through the tube in her mouth.

"Untie my hands!" she ordered, trying to yell. But, the yell came out a breathless, agitated *whoosh*.

"Please, my hands!" The words locked in her thoughts. Only Erin's frenzied breath passed through the intubation tube sticking out of her throat.

"Okay, you're doing good," said a voice in the room. "We were just waiting for you to show us you can breathe on your own. Keep taking deep breaths, and I'll remove the tube."

When Erin looked to the right side of the bed, a big, beautiful, black nurse was looking down at her with a smile on her face that spread from ear to ear. The sun shining through the huge windows behind her caused Erin to squint her eyes to block out the glare.

"Okay now, I'm about to pull the tube out, so take one more deep breath for me. That's right, here we go. Your throat might be a little sore after this," the nurse instructed Erin as she removed the long, hard tube from her throat. "But, just relax and keep breathing. Don't fight it, just let me do the work. I'll give you a little water to soothe the sting in your throat as soon as we're done."

Coughing, gagging and sputtering, Erin finally caught her breath. Her eyes watered, and her body trembled from the traumatic ordeal. Never had she felt so out of control ... or had she? She couldn't remember. The 'why' she couldn't remember was more mind boggling than the physical discomfort she was experiencing. She was sure she would remember anything so horrific.

"Thank you," said Erin. Her raspy, thick voice barely audible. "Please, take these things off my hands! Why am I tied down, and who is Erin?"

Again, Erin didn't know why she was being so adamant about being constrained. What she did know was that not being able to be free was making her crazy. She pulled up her hands and shook her fists to no avail.

"Easy now, I'll get them off." answered the nurse. "And, that's you honey, Erin Berger. That's who you are. Now, we tied your hands because you were trying to pull the tube out of your mouth, and your lungs just weren't ready to breathe on their own. Breathe easy now. I'll untie your hands."

"My name is not Erin!" distraught, she elevated her voice. "I can't remember my name. What's wrong with me? Where am I? Why am I here?"

"It's very common to be a little confused, after what you've been through," the nurse explained. "Don't worry, everything will be straightened out. You'll see. Now, just take another deep breath for me." The nurse's tone had gone from commanding to comforting, her soothing voice attempting to calm Erin. Still, she wasn't feeling calm, and the nurse wasn't giving up any plausible explanations or answers to Erin's questions.

"Can you tell me what year it is?" the nurse asked nonchalantly. Uncertain, Erin cleared her raw throat, her eyes wide with fear.

"1963?"

"Okay," said the nurse. "Now, take a good look at me. Do you remember me?"

"Remember you?" thought Erin. "I've never seen you before in my entire life! At least, I don't think so." Erin looked up at the nurse, her face contorted with confusion and suspicion.

"No," she replied. "Should I?"

"Well, at this point, maybe not. I'm Kerry. I took care of you a few times when you were up on the fourth floor. The doctor is on his way in. Everyone's been waiting for you to wake up. Do you feel like sitting up and talking a little?"

Erin nodded. Her neck was sore, and her back felt like a hot blade was stuck in the middle of it. Her whole body ached.

"Can you tell me where I am and why I'm here?" Erin's facial expression and vocal tone completely changed. She was begging for answers instead of demanding explanations.

"You're at Med General," answered the nurse, as she elevated the head of the bed. "In the Intensive Care Unit. Your heart stopped, sweetie, and you've been in a coma for three days." The look on the nurse's face told Erin that there was more going on than the nurse was saying. Something, no, *everything* felt very wrong.

"You said my name was ... something Berger? Can you tell me my first name again?" Erin's voice quivered as she asked the simple question.

"Yes, your name is Erin." Kerry had seen this many times before. It was nothing out of the ordinary for a comatose patient to lose part of their long-term or short-term memory. But, it was always heartbreaking to see the look on their faces when they realized the obvious.

Whether or not each individual patient had

their memory restored depended on how long their brain had been left without oxygen. And, in Erin's case, the doctors had no idea how long she had been lying there, with no oxygen and no heartbeat.

"Erin, can you tell me what year it is?" the nurse asked, again.

"I told you, it's 1963! Why can't I remember anything? And, just what have I gone through? Please tell me what's going on?" By now, Erin's agitation level had once again escalated to the point of hysteria.

"Okay, Erin. The doctor is on his way, and he'll be able to explain all of this to you. Right now, I'm going to give you a light sedative. Just to relax you."

"What is that? I don't need a ... sedative or whatever you called it!" she tried to shout. "I need to know what's going on! Please! My mind is a blank. What's happened to me?"

As the nurse administered the medication through the I.V., a young doctor wearing blue scrubs and a white lab coat walked in with several residents and an intern.

"Good morning, Erin. I'm Dr. Chan. How are you feeling?"

The nurse leaned over and whispered in his ear, "We're stuck in 1963, doctor!"

"I don't know how I am," answered Erin. "I can't remember anything. I didn't know Erin was my name until the nurse told me. What happened to me?" Frightened and confused, Erin's voice cracked under the stress. The doctor nodded sympathetically.

"This is not uncommon. Your body has had quite a shock. Please try and calm yourself. This memory lapse may take a little while to subside. Hopefully, a little at a time, your memory will come back." The doctor kept talking, but his face manifested a worried scowl. His eyebrows scrunched close together, and he looked like he wanted to cry.

"Your husband is outside waiting to see you," said Dr. Chan. "Should I call him in?"

"Husband?" asked Erin. Her thoughts were erratic and muddled, and her emotions agitated beyond even her comprehension.

What was this idiot saying? What is this husband he's talking about? Is it another kind of doctor or employee, and why is he waiting to see me?

"I don't know what you're talking about!" gasped Erin.

"All right, let's see if we can clear up some of the confusion." Dr. Chan briefly explained to Erin about her husband, Jim. Then, slowly so she could absorb everything being said, informed her about the recent surgery, her discharge, the infection that ensued, the re-admittance into the hospital, and how her heart had stopped and that she had been found non-responsive.

"It appears that somehow your body depleted all of the potassium in your system. That was the cause of your heart stopping."

Erin listened in disbelief, her inner turmoil clear on her face. She didn't understand any of it, and she didn't know what all this had to do with her not knowing who she was. She didn't interrupt, and she didn't ask questions because she didn't know what to ask. All of it was disturbing.

The doctor was talking and talking, but Erin didn't comprehend anything he was saying. It was just a whole lot of "blah, blah, blah".

The nurse walked up to the doctor and whispered, "Her husband is here, doctor."

"Erin, memory loss, be it temporary or permanent, is a common side effect of a patient losing blood supply to the brain. Now, in your case, we don't know how long you were without oxygen. You may recuperate some or all your memories. And, there is the possibility that you won't. But, the key right now is to settle back and let it happen. You can't rush any of this. It just has to take its course, however long that may be. Worrying about it and getting all upset won't make it happen any sooner, if at all. Do you understand?"

Erin never did answer. At that precise moment, Jim walked in and seeing that Erin was awake and talking with Dr. Chan, his lips curled into a wide smile.

"Hi, baby, how are you feeling?" With his arms open, he rushed over to hug and kiss his wife.

Erin abruptly turned her face and defensively pulled away from his embrace. "What are you doing? Who the hell are you?" Her voice, a loud, hysterical screech, her arms out-stretched and stiff, her hands pushing hard against his chest.

"It's me, Jim! Remember? Look at me, Erin.

You know who I am, just look at me."

Crushed, Jim stood up and took a step back. "I'm sorry, baby! Dr. Chan said this might happen, and I know you must be terrified. But, no one is going to hurt you." The pained look on his face reflected the hurt deep in his soul. "You'll start remembering everything, little by little. I promise." The disgusted look on Erin's face transformed into horror, and the fright she exhibited wounded Jim tremendously.

"It's going to take time, Erin," said Dr. Chan. "Just calm down. We're all here to help you through this."

In an effort to lighten the situation, Dr. Chan changed the subject. "Would you like to see the doctor responsible for saving your life? She's been by to see you several times a day, every day since your heart stopped three days ago. But, you'll probably feel like you're meeting her for the first time."

Erin didn't answer. Her throat was dry, and her face warped with fear. But, she nodded, slowly, her mind racing with a million questions when a tiny, young woman with cinnamon-colored skin, almond-shaped eyes, and a radiant smile stepped forward.

"Hi, Ms. Berger! My name is Sara Cabral! And, although you don't know it, we're old friends. Now, other than all this chaos, how are you feeling this morning?"

Erin's confused face softened at the sound of the sweet, melodic voice. Immediately, without thinking, her arms reached up to hug the small woman.

Dr. Cabral leaned over, embraced her patient and, without explanation, both women closed their eyes and tears began to flow. Erin latched on to the young woman with every ounce of strength she had in her painful, weary body. A feeling in her soul revealed that this person was her only link to reality and to her humanity.

This woman had pulled her in from another dimension and brought her back to a world she didn't know. Just maybe, if she held on to her long enough and tight enough, she could and would save her again from the unknown. There was a connection between the two women, so emotional that all the occupants of the room developed knots in their throats and tears in their eyes. Not a whisper was heard as the beat of two hearts bonding was witnessed by all.

A hush fell over the room as the two women clung to each other. Once again, the young intern yearned to give her patient what she needed. This time, with Erin alive, awake, and with full knowledge of who this small woman was and what she was striving to accomplish.

"Thank you, doctor. Thank you for saving my life. I don't think I know what my life is or has been, or that I can ever repay you for what you've done. Just know that I appreciate you, so very much."

"The look on your face is more payment than anyone could ask for," replied Dr. Cabral. "But, there is no payment needed or expected. I only did my job. I just happened to walk in at the right time. I have to tell you, though, you gave me a heck of a hard time. No matter what I did, you didn't want to give up your heartbeats. You would give me one or two beats, then quit. You were quite stubborn and tight-fisted about it. But, you met your match with me because I'm more pig-headed than you could ever be. Seriously, and all kidding aside, I'm so glad you're awake and doing so much better."

Dr. Chan interrupted, "You don't know how fortunate you are that it was Sara who found you. Had it been any other intern, I'm not so sure everything would have turned out the way it did. She had the experience to know exactly what to do. And, when everyone else, including me, felt that it was over, and you had left this world for good, she wouldn't give up. You are here today because of her skill and tenacity as a physician."

"Dr. Cabral, again, thank you. And, now, at the risk of sounding extremely ungrateful, you have to know how frightening all of this is for me. I'm thanking you for saving my life, but I have no idea what my life is. I don't know who I am, anything about myself or how I'm even carrying on this conversation with you.

"I know who these people are," Erin pointed at Jim and Dr. Chan, "only because they have told me. But, I don't *know* them! And, from the look on the nurse's face when she asked, I don't even know what year it is. I'm thinking it's 1963, and I'm in high school."

"Do you recall your high school?" asked Dr.

Chan.

"No," Erin answered, clearly distraught. She turned to Dr. Cabral. "Dr. Chan tells me this is common, but, for me, it's terrifying."

"That's understandable and very normal," replied Dr. Cabral. "Please try not to rush anything. Your whole body has gone through a traumatic ordeal and it's still very early in your recovery. I know it's difficult for you right now, but instead of worrying about what was or might be, let's focus on all the good, right now, at this very moment. The fact that you're alive, talking and moving, is of tremendous significance. You don't appear to have any major, outer physical damage.

"Although we don't know exactly how long you were non-responsive, your physical appearance at the time indicated that it was more than six minutes. Patients undergoing similar experiences have been known to have some paralysis, speech impediments, or worse.

"Let's take it one step at a time. Now that you're awake and responding well, we'll be working with you to recover what you have lost: your memory. But, first things first. Right now, we're planning on moving you out of this Intensive Care Unit into a regular room, where you can have some privacy. Spend some time talking to your husband and maybe the memories will begin to surface. Okay?"

"That's another thing," Erin sobbed. "I don't know anything about a... husband. I have no idea who this man is, and it's frightening. I know I should be grateful. But, I'm not! I feel so lost."

"You're pushing yourself too hard," said Dr. Cabral. "Just try and take it moment by moment. Interacting with your family might trigger some of those lost memories."

"Family? What is that?" Erin inquired. "You mean there's more that I don't remember?"

Dr. Chan and Dr. Cabral began the excruciatingly-slow process of explaining and reassuring Erin. But, to her, nothing was reality. So much of what they were saying sounded like they were talking about someone else, in a language she didn't understand. Gently, and with conviction, Dr. Cabral finally convinced Erin that, with time and a lot of patience, she wouldn't feel as out of touch with the world.

"Try and focus on the positive aspects of all of this," suggested the young physician. "You're out of the coma and communicating logically and without any obvious physical impediments. Give time a chance to catch up with your memories. I know you don't think so, but you aren't alone." hen, with her permission, Dr. Cabral asked everyone to leave the room and proceeded to thoroughly examine Erin.

When the examination was over, Dr. Cabral took Erin's trembling hand and looking deep into her eyes whispered, "Don't be afraid. We're all here to help you through this. Take a deep breath and relax. Don't stress. I'll be back a little later to check on you. Should you need me for anything, I'm here in the hospital and the nurses can easily find me."

After giving specific orders to the nurse, both doctors left the room, promising to return later in the day.

Family

Jim pulled a chair close to the bed. "Don't be afraid. I'm here to help, nothing else. You and I have been best friends for over thirty-five years, and I know everything there is to know about you and your life. Ask me anything. And, if I don't know the answer, I'll make something up. Anything to put that beautiful smile back on your face," he said with a silly grin.

Erin didn't laugh. She didn't even smile. The fear in her chest overwhelmed her, causing her breathing to falter. She forced herself to calm her jitters and took a deep breath.

I don't know you, she thought. *Please, don't get so close and whatever you do, don't touch me!* She closed her eyes, choosing her words carefully. She didn't want to offend this person, but the gravity of the moment dictated that she say something to explain her terror.

"Please, whoever you are, I don't know you. Do you understand?" Erin whimpered. Jim's smile instantly disappeared as he scooted his chair away from the bed and raised his hands, palms open, to show Erin he understood.

"I'm so sorry. I know you're frightened. Yes, I do understand. Trust me, I'll do whatever you say to make you comfortable. I want to help, not hurt you."

At that moment, Erin sighed deeply and just

as she was about to ask about the family that had been mentioned, two women quietly walked in the room.

"Hi, welcome back," the younger of the two said, as she leaned over the side rail of the bed and planted a kiss on Erin's surprised face.

Her pretty, oval face appeared familiar. She had long, wavy black hair, wore bright, red-rimmed glasses that displayed a twinkle in her big, brown eyes, and a cheerful smile that lit up the drab hospital room.

The older woman, a heavily-made-up blonde with puffed-up hair reached over and patted Erin's hand. The stylish, navy blue suit and white gloves she wore accentuated her tall, slim figure.

"Hi, sister," she said. "Some people will do anything to get out of cleaning house and cooking." She smiled wickedly and winked, then stepped back as if she was afraid if she got too close, she might catch something.

"Erin," Jim said. "This little beauty is Elaine, our daughter," pointing to the younger of the two. "And, this is your sister, Betty."

The shocked look on Erin's face disturbed the two women. Elaine looked up at her dad with a million questions in her eyes. He quickly winked at her as if to say, just go with it. She turned back, smiling at Erin, and pleasantly continued with their conversation as if all was well.

"Mom, you call me, Dolly." Unable to control the emotion welling up in her throat, a tear rolled out of the corner of Elaine's eye, slipping down her cheek and finally landing on Erin's hospital gown. "Don't you know me?"

Erin silently watched the tear slide down the young woman's cheek and fall off her face. She then looked down at the wet spot on her chest, to where the tear had landed and gingerly touched the small wet spot on her gown. Erin then reached up gently and lovingly wiped another slow-moving tear from the young stranger's face. "Don't cry...Dolly. I'm going to try hard to remember you, real fast."

Elaine took her mother's hand and kissed the palm, "I know, Mom. You're going to remember. We'll help you.

"To start with, you have a grandson. My son, Sebastian. He's nine and very worried about his Grandma."

Betty stepped forward, and, doing her best to smile convincingly, said, "I'm married and have two daughters. They're away at school. A very expensive, private school! And, my husband is a rocket scientist. A rocket scientist, mind you! Not too many of those around!"

Erin had no idea what the woman was talking about. But, she continued talking and most of the "blah, blah, blah" was about Betty herself and her family. But, in addition, Erin was slowly filled in about many of the close family members she had.

Betty explained that her oldest son, Stephen, lived in Fort Worth, Texas and worked for Bell Helicopter. He had been continually calling to check on her progress. There were so many, cousins, aunts and uncles, it overwhelmed Erin with too many details to absorb.

The day dragged lazily, as the change from ICU took some time. One would have thought that moving a single bed with a patient in it would have been a simple task. To Erin, with her various IV bags hanging from the pole attached to her bed and all the wound packing supplies and drain bags, the undertaking struck her as being quite complicated and the short, cold ride from one floor to another stretched into an eternity.

Nothing in the long halls or on the pale green walls comforted her anxious soul. The nurses and hospital staff attended to their duties efficiently and, hoping not to add to Erin's already-distraught demeanor, quietly and somewhat mechanically settled her into her room.

Once she was hooked up to all the necessary monitors, Erin slowly dozed off. Her severely-tired body felt foreign. Every breath was as if someone else owned it. But, who was she and what did she really look and feel like? Perhaps another entity had moved into her body and was now looking out through her eyes. Maybe that was the Erin they all were talking about.

A few family members stopped by briefly to say hello and wish her a quick recovery. To Erin, it was a blur of unfamiliar faces and confusion, all terribly disappointing and frustrating. She didn't recognize anyone. Their smiles and complex facial expressions seemed out of place. They tried desperately to comfort her, telling her that everything was going to be all right and that soon she would remember everything.

What was this "everything" they were talking about? Only a thick, dense cloud of uncertainty shrouded Erin's existence.

Betty was talking and talking, something she hadn't stopped doing since she walked in. Erin had made a note to ignore all the, "blah, blah, blah", but a sly comment about Erin looking worn out, caught her attention.

Betty handed her older sister a small mirror, suggesting that she do something with her hair and perhaps use a little lipstick. She then unexpectedly reached over and flipped open the bed tray, exposing a larger mirror.

"Here, take a good look at yourself," she ordered. "You look terrible, Erin. You need to take a little pride in your looks, sister. After all, you're laying here not doing anything else. Might as well fix yourself up a little. Everyone wants to come and see if you're okay. You don't want them to see you looking like an old hag."

"Aunt Betty," Elaine interrupted. "Everyone knows what mom's been through. No one expects her to look like a beauty queen. You're fine, Mom. Don't worry, I'll help you with your hair." The look she gave Betty could have killed an ogre, but Elaine held her tongue from saying more, so as not to upset Erin any more than she already was.

Erin took one look in the mirror and the flood of tears that she had been carefully holding back came crashing down like a cascading waterfall. She stared in the looking glass in disbelief. Who was this over-weight, old woman looking back at her? Long, skimpy blond hair with streaks of white and gray surrounded a strange, pale face with deep lines and wrinkles around the mouth. A pair of sad, limpid, green eyes gawked back at her. The dark circles underneath the lower lids appeared to sink the eyes deep into the tired, worn face, enhancing the appearance of a heavy-set cadaver. That, Erin knew, was a complete oxymoron. How she knew, completely escaped her thoughts. And, who the woman gazing out of the mirror was, Erin didn't have a clue.

How was it that she could talk and think, yet her mind was a blank? How did she know it was a blue blanket and a white sheet on the bed? How did her brain know how to make complete sentences? She could think but didn't recognize simple things or people who were supposedly close to her. Nothing made sense.

When they brought her dinner, she absolutely knew the orange was the color "orange", but she had no clue what to do with it. And the red, jiggly stuff in a bowl mystified her. It was familiar, but the name and function escaped Erin.

Jim patiently peeled and sectioned the piece of fruit. Upon biting into it, Erin remembered the taste. Jim called the jiggly stuff, "Jello" and again, after a spoonful, Erin recalled the texture.

That evening, with so many questions and answers that didn't make sense, Erin was exhausted, and cried herself to sleep.

Late that night, after checking in on Erin, Dr. Cabral insisted that Jim go home and have a good night's sleep. She assured him that Erin would be more comfortable if he wasn't in the room watching her sleep.

"Give her some time alone to make the adjustment," she said. "You look like you can use some rest yourself, Mr. Berger."

Against his will and following several arguments, Jim followed the doctor's orders and went home. He didn't sleep well, if at all. He tossed and turned, exasperated. But, if it was better for Erin, then so be it.

At the very least, he was comforted by the knowledge that, presently, she wasn't physically incapacitated. Her organs all appeared to be functioning normally. She was able to talk, and the movements of her limbs didn't appear hindered. Hopefully, he would be able to help her remember who she was, and their life together would continue to move forward. At the moment, finding Erin's identity was the only thing that mattered.

Throughout the night, doctors, nurses and hospital workers continually streamed in to check on Erin's condition and to change her dressings. The most consistent of these was Dr. Cabral, not only in her medical duties but in her warm and caring bedside manner.

"I'll be here until seven in the morning. So, should you need anything, just have them page me. I'll be somewhere in the hospital."

Erin did sleep. Prior to every dressing change, she was given Morphine, causing her to drift off. It was then that all confusion and fear disappeared, allowing her traumatized body and mind to rest and consequently begin to heal.

1967

Early the next morning, the medication nurse walked into Erin's room with her morning meds. "Good morning, Mrs. Berger. How are we feeling today?"

"Good morning," answered Erin.

"Can you tell me what year this is?" asked the nurse.

"Yes, it's 1967," answered Erin. "Where is Jim? Is he somewhere in the hospital?"

"No, Mrs. Berger," the nurse replied. "Mr. Berger went home after you fell asleep last night. He said he would be back bright and early. I suspect he'll be here shortly. Dr. Cabral ordered him to go home and get some sleep. Up until last night, he'd been here with you almost constantly. Now, that's what I call devotion! Sure wish I had someone to care about me that much."

In Erin's mind, all she felt was guilt. Truthfully, she was angry at everyone trying so hard to impose Jim on her. More than that, she was angry at herself for not remembering who he was and how he was as wonderful as everyone said he was.

Yet, somehow, deep in the recesses of Erin's mind or maybe in her heart, there was something warm and comforting about Jim... almost as if she knew him. A certain, familiar feeling that she didn't have with anyone else. When he wasn't in her room,

Erin longed to see him and hear his voice.

No, she didn't remember him, and she definitely couldn't say she loved him. She didn't even know if she liked him. At this point, Erin didn't know what love or like was but, in her soul, she knew him. Whatever he said sounded solid and real. He gave her the impression that if she started to fall, he would be there to catch her and help her through anything. It was as if she had known him all her life.

And, yet, she didn't know what her life was. Just what was it that she was supposed to know about him... about herself? Her blank mind knew nothing, and her heart felt only emptiness.

Currently, the number 1967 was stuck in her head.

"Am I in nursing school?" she wondered, squinted her eyes and shook her head. "What is nursing school? God, I'm so confused!"

Erin took her medication from Nurse Kerry and, as her mind considered all the possibilities, her eyes closed, and she drifted off. When she awoke, Jim was sitting at her side. Her eyes filled with tears, and her voice trembled with emotion at the sight of this kind, caring man.

"Jim," she said.

Jim looked into his wife's eyes, his heart melting.   "You remember me now, Erin?" Hopeful that she would answer favorably, he smiled in anticipation.

"No, I'm sorry," she whispered sadly. "But, I think I know you in here!" and she pointed to her chest. "I can't remember your face, but I sense something warm inside. Do you understand?"

"No. But, I'll take it. That's a start." he said softly. He took her hand and kissed it tenderly.

And, one more time, Erin briskly pulled away. *I'm not that comfortable,* thought Erin. *How dare him take the liberty of touching me?*

Jim didn't flinch. He sat back, slowly and continued looking at his wife.

"You look beautiful when you sleep," he said, smiling sweetly. Hope was written all over his face. The nurse walked in and adjusted the IV tubing. She looked at the two quietly conversing and striving to absorb each other's essence.

"I've never seen so much love in one small room," she said, sniffling. "You two look like two pearls in a clam shell. It's just beautiful." She wiped a tear running out from under her glasses as she walked out of the room. Jim reached over and quickly squeezed Erin's hand reassuringly.

Again, Erin abruptly yanked her hand away, annoyed that once again she was being pushed towards Jim's attentions. She caught the strain in Jim's look, forced herself to smile and quickly changed the subject, "How long have you been here?" she asked.

"Oh, just a little while," he answered. "I didn't want to wake you; you looked so peaceful. How are you?"

"I'm okay. Answer something for me, will you? What year is it?"

"It's 2006."

"2006? That can't be! Why am I stuck in 1967? Tell me about nursing school, what is it?" she asked feverishly.

Jim locked his gaze on her green eyes and smiled. "In '67, you were in nursing school, learning to do what all these nurses do. And, later, you worked in the nursing field for over thirty years. You've delivered more babies than there are bees in a honeycomb. But, your first love, even before, during, and after me, was working in surgery. That's where you were most comfortable and at home, in the operating room.

"Funny thing, while we were dating, I spent more dates sleeping in the recovery room than on the actual date. It seemed that every weekend you were on call; you'd end up getting a call from the hospital and you'd have to go in and work. So, I'd take you in and take a snooze on a gurney in the recovery room while you worked in the O.R. So that's good, you've remembered something about your past."

"No, Jim. I don't remember." Erin responded dismally. "And, I don't understand all those things you're talking about. At least, not completely. Just bits and pieces that don't make sense."

"Well, I do," Jim chuckled. "And, together we'll reminisce, and you'll begin to remember and enjoy our past. You'll see. We've had a fun and exciting life together."

Trapped in nothingness, Erin wanted to grab

on to Jim's memories and happiness. But, her thoughts had no past, her present was terrifying, and her future a frightening blank.

As time progressed, only the year would change and a few of the pieces of the puzzle would drop out of the air and fall into her thoughts. From 1967, she went to 1976 and a small farm with cows, wide open spaces and a limping pig that was in dire need of an injection of some sort. Then, it was 1983, and she remembered a hospital and large bandages on her chest.

True, complete memories didn't come through, only snippets of pictures in her mind, like a puzzle laid out on a table. Her brain feverishly tried to make the pieces fit. Every thought brought anxiety and an uncomfortable, nauseating grip in the pit of her stomach.

Every moment was difficult. People coming in and out of her room, looking at her, looking at parts of her body, asking her questions that she didn't have answers for. From the food they served her to the questions from interns, residents, nurses, techs and visitors about what she remembered, all of it was seriously intrusive.

It was hard enough to allow the nurses to bare her abdomen and change her dressings. But, bathing, she thought, was the worst of all. Just the thought of baring her body to someone she didn't know... and she knew almost no one... caused agonizing humiliation and embarrassment.

Initially, a nursing assistant placed the basin of

warm water on her bed table along with a bar of soap, lotion, powder and towels. Erin blankly stared at everything, the lack of knowledge evident on her tortured face. Jim stepped in, offering to help and insisted that he could guide Erin in the art of bathing. She adamantly protested, "I would rather go without a bath, whatever that is, than let you see me like that. I'm sorry, Jim. I can't do that, I just can't."

Embarrassed, Jim humbly apologized and brought the nurse in to help Erin.

A young nurse by the name of Maria quietly and efficiently took over and explained the process of soaping the washcloth and washing the body parts, starting with the face and working down her body, systematically.

Erin was learning like an innocent child yet feeling the shame of an adult. The humiliation especially shocked her when she untied the hospital gown and let it drop to her lap. What Erin saw not only surprised her but frightened her as well.

"What's wrong with me? Why do I look like this? Is this normal? Does everybody look like this? It's so ugly!"

Patiently, her voice soft as a whisper, Maria explained that at some time in Erin's past, it had been necessary to surgically remove tumors from her breasts.

"From what I was told, you were quite large-breasted, and the surgery left you less than half the size you had been. Due to a wound infection after the surgery, you lost even more tissue, the left breast suffered the worst and was left severely deformed. That's why you look like that."

"That was 1983," Erin whispered, tears forming in her eyes. "I remember the bandages... and pain, but that's all."

Then, with compassion and finesse, Maria continued to instruct Erin with the skill and confidence of the professional that she was.

The greatest degradation consumed Erin when she needed to use the bathroom. She didn't know what her body was going through, only that she felt a tightness in her lower abdomen and a strange twinge in her private parts. Terror-stricken, Erin was sure her life was ending.

"It'll pass," she thought. "I know it will. It has to. Oh, my God, what is wrong with me?" Embarrassed, Erin refused to tell anyone. She held out as long as she could, lying in a semi-fetal position holding on to her abdomen. Because of the large open abdominal wound, it was impossible to lay completely on her side.

As her stomach tightened and the nausea enveloped her, she humbly and with much trepidation, asked Jim to call a nurse in to help her.

Once again, with skill and tact, Maria explained to Erin that her body was letting her know that she needed to evacuate what her system could no longer use, and she described exactly what Erin's body would do and how she needed to respond.

Maria took Erin into the bathroom, lowered the toilet seat and asked her to sit. That action alone bewildered Erin. Maria again, put into words what Erin needed to know in minute detail.

Finally, when Erin felt her body had finished, she was taught to wipe her private areas, from front to back, twice or three times as necessary then flush. And, that was that.

Erin blushed and apologized repeatedly. The shame and agony of humiliation, when Erin smelled the foul odor that wafted up from her body, consumed her and brought her to tears until Maria said, "Every living being does it, and we here in the hospital constantly encourage it. We take in nourishment, our bodies absorb what is necessary to sustain life, and then efficiently push to get rid of the waste. Passing gas and evacuating your bladder and your bowels is part of life and a necessary function. Better out than in, I always say. Besides, you can't go home until you do, and we keep track of such things. If your body doesn't do this, the toxins will kill you. So... listen to your body and follow through accordingly. That's all."

Erin smiled sheepishly and secretly vowed to remember everything she had learned, so as not to have to ask for help with this "procedure" again. Right then and there, Erin decided that Maria was a treasure of information and compassion. Whatever that was.

The Scent of Flowers

Late that afternoon, Elaine and Betty stopped by to check in and bring Erin some flowers, hoping to jar her memory. They told her that deep purple iris and pink and lavender sweet peas were her favorites.

"They're beautiful," she whispered with a blank face and empty eyes. What they were and why these women thought she needed them completely escaped her. But, their loveliness made her grateful for their thoughtfulness. Slowly, she raised them to her face and instinctively inhaled the aroma. Instantly, her expression changed. "My dad! These are my dad's!" Exhilarated, she sat up in the bed and implored her daughter's face for answers.

Betty immediately blurted out the information, oblivious of its impact, shocking her older sister, "No, they're not dad's. He died ten years ago. Why do you remember him and not us? And, how did you know to smell the flowers?"

"I don't remember him. And, I don't know how or why I did that. But, I remember this smell," Erin mused pensively. "Iris, sweet peas, red and yellow Talisman roses and birds of paradise. Is that right? Am I right?"

"Yes, Erin. Dad grew beautiful flowers, and the iris and sweet peas were your favorites. But, I had forgotten how much you loved all his flowers. We hoped these would help jar your memory."

"I don't remember what all those words mean or what they look like," responded Erin. "Just names and this smell. This is so crazy! How can I remember some things so vividly and yet, not remember the simplest things?

"Mother? You said I'm your mother," Erin appealed to Elaine. "Do I have a mother?" Erin was anxious to know and to see everything and anything. Like a ravenous hunger surging through her body, her mind was ready to devour her past.

Betty opened a lavender box she had carried in and proceeded to show Erin pictures of their family. "*WE* had a mother! This is Mom, Dad and me. Mom's dead, too. She died a few years ago. So, it's just you and me, kiddo!"

Erin stared at the photographs through brooding eyes. Her heart broke as she grieved for these people she could not remember and so desperately wanted to recognize. She leafed through photo after photo and not one was familiar.

As she was about to close the lid on the box, Erin eyed a small photograph stuck in the corner of the box. Carefully, she lifted it out, her expression solemn. Whoever he was, it frightened her to the point of hysteria. Why? She had no idea. Only that she hoped she would never see him face to face.

"That's my Godfather, Peter. Do you remember him? Of course, you don't, you don't remember anything! Here's one of you and Mom."

"I'm sorry." Erin cried. "I don't recall either one of them. Why can't I remember? I feel like I keep bumping into a blank wall. I know you are all probably tired of hearing me whine. But, I'm lost in world of nothingness!" What she didn't say was that, although she didn't remember that man, she got a sick feeling in the pit of her stomach when she saw him.

What was it about him that made her heart pound as if it was going to burst out of her body? She didn't know him, and she didn't want to know him. Unfortunately, if he was related to Betty, Erin knew that sooner or later she would have to meet up with him. That thought brought a horribly uncomfortable squeezing to her chest.

"I don't understand it, either," remarked Betty. "Maybe you don't want to remember your life."

"Aunt Betty!" blurted Elaine. "Why would you say that?" Betty didn't answer. She made a snide face and impatiently turned to look out of the window.

"Mom," Elaine's voice trembled. "The doctor said that maybe, if we take you home, it'll trigger more of your memories. You know, seeing familiar surroundings and being among us and your own things at home might help. Physically, you're now stable. Would you like to go home and try?"

Erin's eyes widened when unimaginable fear possessed her body, and she began to shiver as she sunk back, deep into the bed.

Jim had been standing back, allowing the ladies to get acquainted. Seeing the panic in Erin's face prompted him to step forward and intercede.

"Don't be afraid," soothed Jim. "I'll be right there with you the whole time. We'll take it little by little. Trust me!" he whispered softly. "No one is going to hurt you. We're all here to help. This journey is one we'll all make together. You're not alone, Erin."

Erin looked down at her stomach. "What about this? They change me every four hours. Who's going to do this?" In a panic, her tone climbed higher.

"Before you leave the hospital," answered Jim, "with your permission, they'll teach me how to change the dressing. They'll send a nurse to the house a few times to make sure I'm doing it correctly." Jim's voice was strong and reassuring. "I'm willing to learn, if you're willing to let me. I'll change your dressings, as many times as necessary. It'll be okay, I promise. We'll be coming back here to the clinic a couple of times a week, so they can make sure that everything is doing what it's supposed to do. Don't be scared. I'm going to take good care of you. You'll see. Let's give it a shot. Okay?"

"No! It's not okay!" Erin cried. "I can't let a complete stranger look and touch my body, let alone take care of it. I have a hole in my belly that looks and smells like rotten hamburger meat. It's bad enough that the nurses have to deal with it. Look, I appreciate you wanting to care for me, but you have no idea how awful it really is. You haven't seen the hole, and you haven't been close enough to smell it. I can't stand the smell myself. AND, I DON'T KNOW YOU! Why can't you understand that? God, this is so degrading!" Erin covered her face with her hands, her body shaking with distress.

"You remember rotten hamburger meat," snipped Betty, "but you don't remember us? That's weird!"

"What?" asked Erin, her face twisted with the pain of confusion.

"Hamburger meat!" shouted Betty. "You said you smell like rotten hamburger meat. You remember what that is?"

Erin's face immediately changed to a pallid, sad expression. "No," she answered. "I have no idea what that is. I don't know why I said that." She looked up at Jim, imploring his help.

Jim reached out and took her hands in his, lowering them from her face. Oddly, Erin didn't pull away.

"You don't smell!" he murmured. "And, nothing about you is ugly or awful. I know you don't know me or trust me and, to you, I'm some crazy stranger. But, to me, you are the love of my life, and I will take care of you and love you, even if you never love me back again.

"Your wound is open, yes. But, it's clean and what you're smelling is all in your head. The only thing that has an odor is the Betadine solution. It's an antiseptic to keep the wound clean and help you to heal. I can do this for you! I will do this, if you let me. We, as a family, can do so much for you. But, you have to allow it. Give us a chance."

"I'll be there to help, Mom," Elaine chimed in. "Sebastian and I will do whatever we can. We live with you and Dad. As Dad said, we're a family. Let us love and help you. Please!"

"Not me," said Betty, her face gnarled with revulsion. "I pass out at the sight of any blood or guts. And, if it smells, you can forget it. I hate even coming here because I hate hospitals. But, you being at home, all sickly and smelling awful, is an even worse idea. I'm not going to lie, I do smell that hole in your belly, in addition to that stuff they use on you. And it IS really bad. I'll just throw up if I see or smell anything else. Sorry, sis, but don't count on me to do anything like that for you!"

Jim and Elaine turned quickly to look at Betty, daggers being shot at her from both sets of eyes.

"Thanks, Betty. But, no one has asked you to do anything. We don't need or want your help. Elaine and I can and will handle this," retorted Jim, angry and disgusted with Betty's callous, selfish attitude.

"Again, I'm sorry," maintained Betty. "But I'm not going to say things just to get her to go home, so it's easier on you two. Personally, I think she should stay here in the hospital until that hole in her stomach heals up. It's bad enough that she's all mixed up in her head and on top of that she can't do it for herself. And, we're expected to step up and take care of things like smelly, rotten... Well, I have my husband to think about. I just can't get up and leave him hanging! He needs me at home!"

"Once again, no one is asking you to do anything, Betty," Jim answered, his outrage displayed in the tone of his voice.

"PLEASE!" shouted Erin, belittled and humiliated more than she could bear. She didn't belong to or with these people. She didn't belong anywhere. And, despite what they were saying, they were obviously having a hard time dealing with her situation. "I'm lying right here. Has everyone forgotten that? I may not remember anything, but I can still hear, and I do have feelings. No one has to do anything for me. I'm not going to be a burden to anyone. I'll just stay here until..."

"Erin, I'm sorry. You're right, we've been insensitive in talking about you like you're not here," Jim replied, softly. "You never have been and never will be a burden to me. You are *my* wife, and this is between you and me. Maybe you don't quite understand what that means, right now. But, it all boils down to the fact that I love you and I will care for you, today and always. So, let's not involve anyone outside of our family. Let me take you home, and I promise your mind as well as your body will heal. *Please!* Give me a chance to show you the kind of family you have. Elaine and I are *your* family and we *want* to help. No one else needs to do anything. No outsiders!"

"Yes, mom,", Elaine pleaded, sobbing. "We want you home with us. Let us help."

"I'm not an outsider," Betty huffed. "I'm immediate, blood relation. She's my sister, and my advice should be taken into consideration. I'm just thinking what's best for everyone."

Jim ignored Betty and turned to face Erin.

"I've got this, and I'll make sure you're well taken care of. Just trust me."

Hesitantly, and with severe apprehension, Erin finally agreed. She cringed at the thought of leaving the hospital and going somewhere strange with these people she didn't know, especially after everything Betty had said and the way her so-called sister had acted. Erin didn't want to impose on anyone. But, what choice did she have?

She took a deep breath and focused on Jim's eyes.

"I don't know what to do! I'm causing so much turmoil, and I don't want to infringe on anyone's life. But, I don't think I have a choice. And, I guess if you're willing, then I'll do whatever you think is best. It's worth a try," she hesitantly agreed. "Just maybe, it'll jolt my brain into finding the real Erin, or whoever I am."

With a light pat on Erin's hand, and awkward, standoffish hugs to Jim and Elaine, Betty said goodbye, stating, "Well, it's your funeral. When you can't handle it, don't come looking for me, 'cause I'll be the first to say, 'I told you so.'" Elaine kissed her mother's forehead and left to pick Sebastian up from school and to get things ready at home for Erin.

Jim left the room to sign Erin out of the hospital but not before he bent over, quickly kissed her cheek, and squeezed her hand saying, "Everything is going to be okay. You'll see. I won't let you down, I promise."

Uneasy, she puzzled over everyone's

comfortable use of public displays of affection. These people hugged and kissed her and each other with the ease of a hand-shake. Personally, she would have preferred that hand-shake.

Erin lay there, her eyes closed, petrified, pondering what the next few hours or the next few days would be like. Getting to know these supposed family members was going to be difficult and uncomfortable for all of them.

She heard a clatter by the door and her eyes flew open. An EKG technician with a worried look on her face had walked into the room.

"Ms. Berger," she said. "I'm sorry to disturb you. But, could I ask a favor, please?"

"Sure, what is it? What can I do for you?" asked Erin, looking a bit perplexed.

"Ma'am, I know this is going to sound strange, but could I touch you? Your hand, I mean?" the tech timidly asked.

"Touch me? Do you need to do an EKG on me?"

"No ma'am," she replied, nervously looking back at the door. "I heard that you died, and they brought you back. Everyone says it was a miracle. So... if I could please just touch your hand? And, if you could possibly tell me what you saw when you were on the other side? Please, maybe some of your good luck will rub off on me."

"Oh, sweet lady," Erin stammered. "I'm no one special. The one you should admire is Dr. Cabral. She's the heroine in this story. Not me. She brought me back. It was her skill and knowledge and her tenacity that saved my life. And, actually, the way I see it, she didn't save my life; she gave it back to me. From what I understand, yes, when she found me I was dead, and she just wouldn't accept that. It was her heart that brought me back. So, please, touching me won't have any effect on you or your life. Really!"

"Please," begged the technician. Her eyes swimming in tears and her timid voice cracking with emotion. "Just let me touch your hand. Everybody in the hospital is calling you the 'Thanksgiving Miracle Lady'. Please, Ms. Berger?"

Erin's face flushed with embarrassment and frustration at the request. *This is crazy*, she thought. *But, this woman adamantly believes touching me might enhance her life. I'm nobody, and it's ludicrous, but how do I say no and not hurt her feelings?*

"I'm happy to hold your hand, Miss. But, just as a patient that's grateful to be alive. Nothing more. As for what I saw and heard, except for a blinding white light, I don't remember anything. My memory has been erased, and I now don't even know who I am. My mind is a complete blank. So, you see, I'm not a miracle. I'm just a patient that *coded*. My heart stopped working for a little while, that's all. But, you're right about being blessed or lucky. I'm lucky that Dr. Cabral found me when she did. She is the miracle worker. Thanks to her, I'm here talking to you."

Erin held out her hand and, as she took the woman's hand in hers, she felt a warmth that went straight to her heart. The woman fell to her knees and began sobbing uncontrollably.

"Thank you, thank you so much. You can't imagine how much this means to me. I could lose my job if my supervisors found out I did this. They would claim that's it's unethical and unprofessional. They'd say it was an invasion of your privacy. They're telling all the employees not to bother you and to proceed as normal according to hospital policies. But, I just had to see you," she cried.

"Not to worry," Erin's voice softened. "The only thing that's happened here is that you've come to wish me well and bid farewell to a patient who's going home. Thank you for coming to see me, ...?"

"Annie, my name is Annie."

"Thank you, Annie. And, good luck."

"No, thank you. And, I *will* have good luck now, Ms. Berger! I know I will!" The technician kissed Erin's hand and left with the EKG machine clattering as noisily as when she had walked in the room, leaving Erin contemplating what had just transpired.

Erin wondered if this was just a sample of what was yet to come. How many more people would want to know what it was like to die and yet escape the Grim Reaper's clutch without physical damage and live to talk about it? Was this another facet of this tremendously horrific nightmare?

Going Home

After a few minutes, Jim walked in with his usual smile and a nurse at his side pushing a wheelchair. "Behold your chariot and humble servant, your Highness! Can I help you get dressed?"

"NO! Sorry... the nurse can help me. Okay?" The frightened look on Erin's face caused Jim to take an immediate step backward. Once again, she didn't understand a word of what Jim was saying. Chariot, servant, high ... what was that? Why was he talking to her like that?

"As you wish. But, they're going to change your dressings before we go. So, I'll need to be in here to learn how, before you get dressed. I brought you a nightgown, your robe, slippers, and some undies. I hope they're all right? I've had your things in a bag in the trunk of the car. You know, just in case they let you come home, I'd be prepared."

Erin emptied the bag and stared at the lingerie; wondering about a particular piece of clothing in her hands. *What in the world is this triangle with strings*? She thought. *And, what am I supposed to do with it?*

The nurse stepped up with an armful of supplies. She winked and took the strings out of Erin's hands and set them aside, then she proceeded to inject the pain medication in the I.V. tube. Next, she prepared the supplies, lifted Erin's hospital gown just enough to expose her abdomen, covered Erin's private areas with the sheet and began to teach Jim how to handle the dressing change.

Erin closed her eyes tight and pretended Jim wasn't in the room. She felt silly, but it worked to help keep her nerves calm and her pride intact.

As soon as the wound was cleaned, packed and covered, the nurse turned to Jim and declared," I'll take it from here and help you dress, Ms. Berger." Jim took the hint and offered to step out for a moment while Erin prepared herself for the ride home.

The nurse then gathered the silky strings and explained, "This here is called a *thong,* Ms. Berger. It's what all the women are wearing instead of panties. It makes you feel feminine. You know, it's sensual or sexy or something like that. Anyway, let me show you how this works." and patiently, the nurse helped Erin.

At one point, Jim overheard Erin asking, "This string goes where?" and the nurse giggled and whispered something inaudible. She helped with the nightgown and asked her to sit on the side of the bed.

"There's one more thing you need to do before you can be discharged, Erin. Physical Therapy will be here any moment. They need to make sure you can walk up those two stairs at the entrance to your house. It won't take long. Here's Tim now."

"Good morning, Ms. Berger." Tim greeted Erin with a smile full of crooked, yet pearly, white teeth.

"Are you ready to take a walk with me? I just need to make sure you can climb a couple of stairs with no problem, and then you can get out of here. I'm sure you're tired of our delicious hospital food by now."

Tim helped Erin to stand, holding on to a walker. He gently tied a long, scarf looking piece of material around her waist and knotted it at her back, where he held on tight.

"Okay, now, let's walk over to that door in the hall where the staircase is located. I just need to have you climb and come down a few stairs. You know, like you would at your home. You might be a little stiff at first, since it'll be the first time since your incident. But, we'll take it slow."

To say Erin was stiff was an exaggerated understatement. She had been able to walk to the bathroom, slowly. But, to get her legs to climb one small stair was almost impossible. Her head was thinking it, her lips were saying it, but her legs didn't feel like they wanted to cooperate.

"Hold on to the banister, put one foot on the stair, push your body and pull yourself up," Tim instructed. "You can do it. Your brain just has to tell your legs how. Don't be afraid. I'm right here and I promise I won't let you fall. Just believe in yourself. Come on, let's try."

Erin, perspiring profusely, used every ounce of strength and determination to take that first step. Trembling, and in agonizing pain from her abdomen and the lack of use of her lower extremities, she willed herself to accomplish her feat. One step at a time, she climbed ever so slowly. But, she did it.

"Okay, great, now let's turn around, slowly, carefully." Tim guided. "That's right, I'm right behind you. Now, let's go down. It's not as difficult as going up, but it's no piece of cake. You still need to be cautious. Easy, now, hold onto the banister."

Erin didn't say a word. She was doing well just to breathe normally. So focused was she at performing her task that she would find herself holding her breath as she carried out Tim's instructions.

Softly, Tim would say, "Breathe, Erin." And, they would continue. Once down, she latched onto the walker and slowly walked back to her room, her legs trembling from the strain.

"You'll be able to take the walker home with you. It'll be a big help. Use it however long and whenever you need it," Tim said. "Okay, Ms. Berger, you're good to go. I'll sign the papers, and you can be on your way."

The nurse assisted Erin into the wheelchair and, smiling at the accomplishment, they met Jim out in the hall.

"I never would have thought that something so easy could be so difficult." Erin commented. "How could I forget how to walk and use my legs to climb a few stairs? I'm sure people do it all the time without even thinking about it. It's just something one does automatically, right? Incredible!"

"You'll get better at it, you'll see" assured the nurse. "It just takes practice. The more you do it, the easier it becomes until you can do it without thinking."

It was the beginning of Erin's journey into her new life. Terrified, she squeezed her eyes shut, took a deep breath and said a silent prayer to whomever or whatever in the universe was listening.

"Please, help me to remember and keep me safe and cooperative, for Jim and *his* family's sake."

The short ride home was basically uneventful, except for a strange feeling that Erin had done this before.

As Jim stopped for a red light at the corner, a colorful scene flashed in Erin's mind: *She was in a small car with a man in an odd-looking hat driving. He was talking and talking, but Erin didn't understand a single word.*

They traveled down a dirt road and followed a river, lined with huge, beautiful trees. There were no street lights and only one sign that read, "Fechenbach/Colenberg Am Main". And then, the strange recollection was gone.

Erin barely took a breath as Jim drove up to the little yellow house with the palm trees arching over the drive way. The bright magenta bougainvillea lining the front porch welcomed Erin home. But, warmth and comfort were a far cry from what Erin's body was feeling.

Her heart pounded as small beads of

perspiration formed on her forehead and upper lip. The back of her neck was damp and her wet, clammy hands trembled. Erin's thoughts whirled with so much insecurity and fear that her breath escaped from her body, short and shallow. Paralyzed with fear, her entire body ached.

She didn't have any options. They all said this was *her* family and *her* home. Where else could she go? Who could she turn to? She knew no one else. The only person that instilled security in Erin was Dr. Cabral, and she couldn't very well ask her to take her home. So, this was it.

She glanced up and down the street and, when she turned her head she found Jim, patient and reassuring, standing ready to open her car door.

"It's okay, you're home, now. Don't be scared, I'll help you find your way," his voice, soft and kind. He took Erin's hand and, with a gentle yet firm grip, helped her out of the car and up the steps.

Elaine, smiling, stood holding the front door to the house, open. "Welcome home, Mom."

"Aunt Betty went home, so you can relax. It's just us. And, you mustn't mind her. She doesn't really mean any harm. She's just a little self-centered. The most important person in her life is her. Can I get you something to eat or drink?"

"Thanks, but not just yet," answered Erin as she walked across the threshold and stood in front of an old, tattered, over-stuffed, blue recliner. Looking around, taking in all the furniture and the pictures on the wall, she hoped to absorb the warmth of this home.

Except for her eyes, her body was motionless. She stood for a long while, staring. Her breathing quickly accelerated, and her heart pounded like thunder deep in her chest.

"Would you like to sit down or maybe you'd like to go to your room and lie down?" asked Elaine.

"No, thank you. Not right now," she replied.

"Is something wrong? Do you feel all right, Mom?" Elaine's eyes were swimming in tears, worry lines etched on her young face.

"I... uh, need to use the restroom," whispered Erin.

"Do you need help?" asked Jim. "I can help you."

"No! I don't need help. I can manage myself." Erin didn't take a step, she just kept looking around. Lost. She leaned over towards Elaine and softly, choking on her words, said, "I don't know where it is."

Elaine quickly took her mother's hand and quietly answered, "Come, I'll show you."

At that moment, Jim and Elaine exchanged glances, and they knew it was going to be a long, hard transition for Erin as well as for all of them. No matter how much love they felt and were willing to show her, this would be a difficult journey. Patience would play the most important role, along with all the love they could muster.

Stoic and brave, Erin's facial expression showed no fear. But, her demeanor was cautious and guarded as her gait demonstrated her wary steps. Her eyes absorbed everything in her path in total silence.   She followed Elaine down the short hallway, entered the bathroom and as she closed the door, the click of the lock resounded loud and clear. A long, slow sigh was heard, followed by the sound of gentle, running water and quiet weeping.

Uncomfortable moments passed and finally they heard Erin's soft voice, "Elaine?"

"Yes Mom, are you all right?"

"Elaine, there's no paper!"

"Oh, my gosh, Mom! I'm so sorry!" Elaine was mortified. "Mom, just look in the cupboard, to your left, under the sink. There should be some there. Did you find it?"

"Yes, thank you."

Jim and Elaine, for the first time, began to really understand the discomfort and insecurity Erin was probably feeling. Not only did she not recognize them, she didn't know the house or where anything was. Erin was alone in an empty world with nothing and no one familiar to hold on to.

Jim collapsed on the sofa, his head dropping down and his face sinking into his hands. His shoulders rounded with the weight of the challenges before him and his family, as well as the responsibility of guiding his wife through the upcoming difficulties.

"Give her time, Dad," Elaine consoled. "We'll get her through this, together."

At that moment, the front door flew open

and in ran curly, red- headed Sebastian. "Where's Grandma? Is she here yet?"

"Easy, Bubba! (Bubba was Erin's nickname for her grandson). She's in the bathroom," answered Jim. "Remember, now, she doesn't remember who we are. So, we have to be patient with her. We don't want to scare her. She's already a bit overwhelmed. Go slow, okay? And be careful with her stomach!"

Erin walked back into the living room, took one look at Sebastian and asked, "Bubba?"

Sebastian ran over and bear hugged Erin.

"Easy, partner. She just got out of the hospital," said Jim, as he reached out to protect Erin.

"Grandma, they said you didn't remember anyone. But, you know who I am?"

"I recognize you! I don't know who I am or what year it is, but I recognize you from the pictures. Incredible, huh?" Erin felt a warmth but could not get herself to return the hug. She stood there, frozen with her Bubba's arms around her waist and his head on her bosom.

Sebastian looked up at her with big green eyes that begged Erin to love him. After several seconds of discomfort, she lightly placed one hand on his shoulder and the other on his head and tousled his rumpled hair. It wasn't much, but the nine-year-old little boy took it as a sign of affection, something she hadn't shown anyone else. And, that was enough for the moment.

Learning

"There's plenty of food in the fridge, Mom," said Elaine. "A few of your favorites. So, whenever you're hungry, just let Dad know. He makes a delicious hot chocolate that you just love. I'll bet he could be persuaded to make some for you.

"I have no idea what my favorites are," countered Erin. "I don't even know what I like and don't like, so anything will be fine. But, I'm not hungry right now. Thank you, anyway."

"Sebastian and I are going to the mall to get him some shoes, continued Elaine. "You and Dad could use some 'alone' time to kind of get reacquainted. So, enjoy and we'll be back in a couple of hours. If you need anything, just call me."

"You said to call you 'Dolly'." Erin quizzically looked up at her daughter. "What else will I call you?"

"Right, Mom," replied Elaine casting a perplexed look at Jim. Immediately, she realized that presently they would all need to provide better, more informative explanations, when speaking with her mother. "If you need or want to get in touch with me while we're out, you can use the phone, Mom. You know?"

The look on Erin's face told everyone she didn't know.

"I'm here, and you have a cell phone. We all do, and all the numbers are already in there," said

Jim.

"A *what* phone?" asked Erin, confused. Her eyebrows scrunched together, and deep lines were etched on her forehead.

Jim showed Erin her cell phone and proceeded to explain all about how house phones or 'land lines', as they were now called, were almost a thing of the past. A smile crept up on her face when she saw a picture of she and Jim on the face of the cell phone. Still, she had no idea how a phone worked or how they had so much information stored up in such a small space. It was just another of the many things that she was going to learn from these sweet, strange people. *Her family.*

Elaine and Sebastian kissed and hugged Jim and Erin goodbye and left Jim to teach Erin.

The lessons began and Erin, wide-eyed and child-like, enthusiastically started the learning process. First and most importantly, there was the layout of the house and her bedroom. She walked gingerly through the house and timidly looked through her drawers trying desperately to familiarize herself with *her* belongings.

Slowly, more and more pieces of the puzzle began to take their place. The pieces still didn't fit together, but definite pictures were beginning to form in her head.

Jim gave her space and allowed her to introduce herself to her surroundings. Alone, she explored all the rooms of the house, opening cupboards and drawers. Every so often, a smile would cross her lips. Whether she remembered something or not, Jim didn't ask. He made his presence known but gave her time to inhale the aromas of their home and embrace the warmth of their life together.

Erin caressed many of the objects in her room, her toiletries, makeup and perfume. She opened a bottle of perfume and made a quirky face, "Whew, this is awful! What is it? It's not mine, is it?"

Jim laughed, "Yes, it is, and you used to love the way it smelled. It's your favorite scent. You know, supposedly, it makes you smell good. But, I'm so glad you don't like it anymore, 'cause I've always hated the odor. We can get rid of it, right now." Gently, he lifted the small bottle from Erin's fingers and threw it directly into a small trash can.

"That's the end of that smell," Jim laughed.

Although she found herself becoming engrossed in exploring, she kept a watchful eye on Jim. Out of the corner of her eye, she could see him watching her actions, following her around with his eyes and looking like an unwanted puppy.

"Is this where I'll be sleeping?" she asked.

"Yes, this is our bedroom," Jim replied. He reached over and picked up a wedding picture of the two of them. "Look, this is what we looked like thirty-five years ago. I'm still the same handsome devil, don't you think?" With a wink and a smile, he hoped his question would lighten the mood. But, Erin looked annoyed.

"You're not planning to sleep here, are you?"

It was more of a statement than a question.

"If you're worried I'll take advantage of you, I won't. But, this is where I sleep. Look, it's a Queen Size bed, and there's plenty of room for both of us. I promise I won't hurt you or try anything uncomfortable for you. But, I'd like to be right here, just in case you need anything. I can answer questions, tell jokes, sing you to sleep, but I have to warn you, I can't carry a tune, and I snore. Any one of those actions just might jar your memory, and I want to be here to help you through it." The silly look on Jim's face made Erin smile, despite her apprehension.

"Funny," Erin smirked. "The nurses didn't sleep with me, or in my room, even, and, I did quite well."

"That's because they're nurses and confident about how they do things" Jim said with conviction. "I'm *pretending* to be a nurse and not so confident, so I have to be right here with you. Just in case you need me. Or anything!" With a wicked smile, he winked again.

Looking at her uneasy expression, the smile melted away and a serious look took its place. "Please, don't be nervous. Nothing is going to happen that you don't want. First of all, I love and respect you and would never take advantage of you. Second, you're recovering. I'm here to take care of you. If it makes you feel any better, we can leave the door open. Elaine and Sebastian are just down the hall from us, should you have need. But, one thing's for sure; I'm sleeping here in *our* bed, *with* you."

"I'm not trying to be impossible, Jim. But, this anxious feeling of not knowing or remembering overwhelms me sometimes. I guess to be truthful, always. I can't just put it aside, hard as I try.

"I'm somewhat comfortable with you. And, I feel that I know Bubba. But, I don't really remember either one of you. I know it sounds crazy, and maybe that's what I am, crazy, 'cause I can't explain it.

"I don't even know how to comb my hair. The nurse had to show me how to brush my teeth..." By now, Erin was gritting her teeth and tears were streaming down her cheeks. "Can you imagine how humiliating it is to have someone try and teach you how to wipe your rear end when you use the toilet? It's degrading! I can walk, and I make pretty good sense when I talk, yet, I don't know how to care of myself. I'm afraid of you getting in the bed with me, but I don't know why. Nothing makes sense. I'm sorry, I'll try and be more cooperative."

"I'll teach you everything you need to know, and I'll guide you, my sweet." Jim's silky voice attempted to soothe Erin's anxiety. "We've been together over thirty-five years. There is nothing that we haven't done together. I understand that this is all new to *you*. And, until you are comfortable with me, patience will be number one. Promise. Just let me care for you. Like a friend, like a nurse. Nothing else."

"Do me a favor, will you?" Erin pleaded. "Don't call me 'your sweet' or 'baby' or 'honey', please? I don't even like you calling me 'Erin', because I don't know who Erin is. But those other names just irritate me. So, don't call me those names - at least, not for a while. The thought of belonging to you or anyone just doesn't sit well with me. I don't even belong to myself right now."

Jim's smile reappeared, "I'm sorry. It'll get better, and I'll try not to push. I know it's hard. Just don't give up. Please!"

Erin found her way to a door in the bedroom and as she opened it, Jim quickly spoke up, "That's my closet, and you're welcome to look around. Yours is on the other side."

"Closet?" She inquired.

"Go ahead, open the door," Jim responded. "It's where you keep your stuff."

She walked over, opened the door and stood there dumbfounded at all the contents of the small room. Clothes, shoes, boxes and bags all neatly stacked on shelves and on the floor. Strange clumps of hair sitting on white heads with blank faces stared back at her.

"What is all this?" she asked, looking back at Jim.

"These are all your things."

"What did I do with all this ... stuff?" she asked with a scared look on her face.

"You lived," Jim answered. "And, you enjoyed every bit of your life. Our life. We had fun."

"What are these things," Erin's eyes squinted together fully perplexed as she pointed to the heads of hair.

"Those are your wigs, love! Oh, sorry! *Erin*. As

you already noticed, you don't have much hair. That's due to the fact that you were very ill at one time, and the medication and treatments they gave you made you lose all your hair. When it finally grew back, it didn't all come back. You wear these on your head because they make you feel better about how you look."

Erin walked over to a small, ornate dresser. She opened a drawer and found small containers of creams and lotions, facial wipes and bottles of liquids and tubes of tinted creams.

"That's more of your make-up. And, stuff to make your face and body soft." Now, Jim blushed. "I don't know too much about how those things work, but I'm sure Elaine can help you with it."

Erin opened the next drawer and pulled up some lingerie. More of the 'thongs' and some weird looking things with straps and thick, hard bumps. "What are these?"

"Those are your bras. You know, ladies wear them, on top," Jim explained as he pointed to his chest.

"They're hard and lumpy. I wear these?" she asked.

"They call them 'padded bras'. I think they make you look more... even. When you got sick, they removed that part of your body. You know your bosoms? So, you say these make you look better in your clothes. You know, symmetrical. Even!"

"My deformed chest." Touching her chest, Erin's face searched Jim's for answers. "My breasts don't look the same."

"After the surgery, you developed an infection, and it ate away at the remaining breast tissue." Jim didn't fumble with his words. He explained simply what he knew. "Your left breast took the brunt of it, causing a severe deformity. When you wear these bras, it evens you out, so your clothes look better. At least that's what you say. Something about *draping*, I think you call it. I don't know anything about that sort of stuff. I just think you're beautiful with or without these things."

Blushing, all Erin could think of saying was, "Thank you."

She remembered the nurse telling her something similar. So, she tucked that bit of information about the bras, in the back of her mind. Clothing was something she would ask Elaine about, later.

Trusting

The days that followed proved to be stressful for all. Especially Erin. But, she didn't give up and her family stayed by her side, coaching, teaching, loving.

The home nurse came to the house and went over the aesthetics of the dressing change with Jim, and how to nurse the wound. It was something he was already quite familiar with.

Erin still had drains in place to eliminate the accumulated drainage from the infection. Consequently, the nurse attached a kind of vacuum to the wound to remove the fluid and, the moment she turned it on, Erin screamed in pain. So much so that Jim demanded that she immediately remove the contraption from Erin's wound.

The same type of vacuum had been used in the hospital, but a stronger pain medication had been administered prior to the dressing change. Therefore, Erin had not experienced such profound torment. At that precise moment, Jim decided such a procedure would not be used again.

Jim later commented that he thought the whole neighborhood probably heard the commotion. He kidded that they probably thought that Erin was beating him up for his terrible cooking.

When the nurse was finished with her duties, he looked the nurse square in the face and said, "Thank you so much for coming. But, it's not necessary for you to come again. I can do this for my wife. Tomorrow, we have an appointment at the clinic. I think we can take it from here. Again, thank you for your time."

Against her will and with much arguing, Jim escorted the nurse to the door. "I don't mean to be rude. But, I'm sure you have other patients who need your care. As I said, I can take care of my wife. Thank you so much for your help." And, that was that.

From that day forward, Erin watched her husband wash his hands, don his disposable gloves, and proceed to care of her like a skilled health-care professional. The pain continued to be excruciating, but it had nothing to do with his technique. His touch was light and steady. No doctor or nurse, watching his procedures, could have ever guessed that he hadn't been doing it for years. The only difference was that he always ended the procedure with a wink and a smile saying, "You're dressed for the ball, your Majesty".

Relaxing and allowing this man to see parts of her body in its ugliest, raw form was a most difficult task for Erin. To watch him remove the blood-saturated gauze and clean out the gaping hole in her belly, carefully, so as not to disturb anything that was trying to heal, was degrading and humiliating, to say the least. Erin continued to sense that there was an odor and that in itself mortified her.

Yet, Jim's facial expression never showed anything but tenderness and concern. He reiterated over and over that what she was smelling was the antiseptic solution he used to irrigate the wound. Nothing else.

Still, it was Erin who was self-conscious and who felt vulnerable, during the dressing changes and, even more so, when it came to bathing.

Elaine had offered to help with her bath, late in the evening, after she got home from work, but Elaine had her hands full looking after Sebastian.

Jim just took control of the conversation and said, "I'll help your mother with her bath in the morning after she has her breakfast. That way, she can feel fresh and squeaky clean all day long. Not to worry, I've got this."

Conflicted Feelings

Jim's attitude irritated Erin beyond comprehension. She knew she should be feeling gratitude for all he did and wanted to do for her. But, his management of every situation, without considering her feelings, aggravated her to the point of insanity.

He never asked, "Is this okay with you?" or "Do you mind if I take care of this?" His approach was always that of "I'm in charge and this is what we're going to do." No questions asked.

I'm not a child who needs direction, she thought. *I've lost my memory, not my thought process.*

Because she was unable to get in the shower due to her open wound, she would close the lid on the commode and sit facing the sink. Jim would fill the wash basin with warm water and allow her to wash as much as she could manage privately. As soon as Erin would cover up sufficiently, he would go in and wash her back and her legs from the knees down to her feet.

Kidding, with his big smile, Jim would say, "I'll wash down as far as possible and up as far as possible. *You* wash possible!" and then laugh. It was always Erin who had the difficulty, not Jim.

Little by little, she began to relax with him. She grew to depend on him and no longer shied away from his touch. She still blushed, but Jim said it was part of her charm. And, after her bath, she allowed him to rub her back with lotion and massage her lower legs and her feet. Gratefully, Erin accepted Jim's thoughtfulness and, because it felt so utterly exquisite, she pushed her modesty aside and just enjoyed the pampering.

But, inadvertently, the feeling of always being in his control began to fester. The conflict, in her head and in her heart, became a daily struggle. At times, she loved and appreciated his help and his care. But, at times, the fight to keep her thoughts and anger to herself, brought her to tears. Still, she said nothing for fear of hurting the gentle man who always put her comfort and well-being before anything and anyone else. Especially, himself.

Ornaments

Christmas was approaching and there was a flutter of activity in the house. Erin didn't know what it was all about but avoided getting in the way and asking any questions. She merely sat and watched as Jim, Elaine and Sebastian opened large boxes of glittering decorations. Where they were going to be put was a question that answered itself when Jim brought in the large evergreen tree. The fresh scent filled the small living room and embraced Erin's senses.

"Christmas is your favorite time of the year, Mom," explained Elaine. "These ornaments have always been very special to you. You've been collecting them since you were a little girl.

"Dad and I thought they might bring back some memories of Grandma, Grandpa, and your family times together." Elaine then placed a large, long box on the ottoman in front of Erin. When she lifted the top off the box, Erin's face lit up and a hushed gasp escaped her.

The glass orbs felt delicate to the touch and, when the light filtered through the window, they sparkled with a divine brilliance. Little by little, lights were added to the tree, and, one by one, the ornaments were hung in strategic places on the boughs.

Several small boxes encased crystal icicles of

varying sizes and lengths displaying unique etchings. Erin couldn't take her eyes away from their beauty.

"Those were gifts from your brother," whispered Jim.

"My brother," questioned Erin. "I thought Betty said there were just two of us."

"Now," answered Jim. "Your brother, Ed, passed away several years ago. Here's a picture of him." Jim handed Erin a photograph of a handsome, tall man with jet black hair, olive skin, and a smile that lit up his surroundings.

"He's gorgeous," Erin said. "Who's the good-looking guy with him?"

"That's Sam, his husband," replied Jim.

"Husband?" asked Erin, a bit perplexed.

"Yes, Ed and Sam lived in San Francisco and were together for about thirty-one years. The last five, as a married couple. When California allowed same-sex marriages, they jumped at the opportunity and immediately got married.

"Your brother was a beautiful, loving, educated man with a voice that would vibrate in a church. You and he were extremely close. You talked on the phone at least twice a week and each time for a minimum of two hours. What you found to talk so much about was a mystery to me, and Sam. But, talk you did."

"Why didn't Betty tell me about him?" Erin inquired.

"Betty didn't accept his lifestyle, and she made his existence and Sam's miserable. She told him to change his ways or forget he had a sister. She called the shots and lost the love of the most caring soul she'll ever know.

"It wasn't until after he passed away that she realized what she had missed. But, then it was too late. And, to this day, it eats away at her conscience. So, she figures if she never talks about him, nothing ever happened, and he never existed. It doesn't make sense, but you know how your sister is."

No, thought Erin, *but I'm learning.*

Erin's thoughts whirled in her head. Fuzzy images and sounds invaded her mind.

A little store, crowded with Christmas trees and hundreds of boxes filled with ornaments of all shapes and sizes, glistened in the afternoon sun. Christmas music filled the air and shoppers of all ages talked, laughed, and handled all sorts of decorations, large and small and thoroughly enjoyed their shopping.

Her brother, Ed, was kneeling on the floor, looking under one of the decorated trees, attempting to reach a long, flat box leaning against the wall behind the tree.

"I've almost got it," he informed her. "It's the crystal icicles I've been telling you about. It's the last box, and they're exquisite."

"These will add to our collection, and our trees will give the most beautiful twinkles ever."

"Get your butt up off the floor, or your back will go out and you'll be twinkling from your bed. You're not as young as you think you are. Come on,

old man, get up from there."

"I'm not old, just well-seasoned," Ed answered, winking at Erin with a lilt in his voice.

Her eyes filled with tears and the memory of the brother she loved so much, embraced her soul. Her first memory of family love. She didn't remember much about him, but the recollection of shopping at Christmas time in San Francisco was vividly colorful and it captured her soul. She would hang on to this piece of the puzzle because it formed a definite picture that tugged at her heart.

Sitting there, watching her husband, daughter and grandson milling around the tree, adding to the beauty of the activities, Erin experienced the empty spaces of her heart being filled with the joy of *this* family. They were happy just to be together, laughing, talking and explaining to her their traditions and so many of the things that Erin, herself, used to do to make the holiday special. She was learning.

They talked about the foods she prepared and the special sweets she would put out, just for the holiday.

They commented on Betty and her family coming over for the holidays, for all of about an hour. Just long enough to eat and pick up their gifts, then leave. All because they had so many invitations and obligations to fulfill. Betty said she was such a popular person and needed to attend everyone's functions, so as not to offend anyone.

Wet with salted tears, Erin's eyes closed as she tried and failed to remember their joyous memories.

"Don't cry, Grandma," Bubba whispered. "It's okay not to remember. We'll do stuff that will make you happy, and you'll have fun with us 'cause we're a fun family. You'll see."

"Sure, we will, Bubba," Erin answered. "Already we're making new memories, and I'm crying because I am happy."

The truth was, Erin really was happy, though still confused in her emotions and her thoughts. But, if they didn't give up, neither would she.

Friends

Early one morning, Erin and Jim made the trip to the clinic and were sitting quietly, waiting to see Dr. Cabral. They passed the time watching patients and their families come and go from their scheduled appointments, when a young woman came running towards them. She approached Erin and knelt down in front of her, taking her hands in her own.

"Senora, you died on me. They told me you died. You are the Miracle Lady everyone in the hospital is talking about. You died!"

Frightened, the young woman's face in her lap, Erin looked up at Jim. Her face covered with so many questions, yet speechless. Erin was unable to find the words to say to the young woman.

"Erin," said Jim. "This is Lilly. She was your nurse when you were admitted into the hospital. She took care of you almost every day."

"Hi, Lilly. Don't cry. I'm okay." Erin softly uttered.

"I know, but you died and now you're here," cried Lilly. "I thought I would never see you again. You were my favorite patient. I took care of you, and you died while I was on vacation. When I came back, they said you were gone."

Uncomfortable, Erin stroked the young woman's hair and said, "Yes, but I'm fine. Look at me, I'm okay."

"Oh, my God! I'm so happy to see you again. I can't stay, I've just had lunch, and need to get back to work," said Lilly. "I just happened to come through the clinic on my way back... and here you were. I couldn't believe it was you. I'm so happy I got to see you again and that you're okay.

"I have to get back upstairs; as I said, I'm on duty. But, I'm so glad to see you. Please, come and see me when you come to clinic. I'd love to visit and talk to you again. Please, Senora."

"Yes, I will, and thank you for taking such good care of me." After she left, Jim filled Erin in with all the particulars regarding Lilly and the relationship she and Erin had formed.

Lilly, along with Kerry, the nurse in ICU, had taken care of Erin up on the fourth floor after she was admitted for the infection. For some reason, Lilly took an immense liking to Erin and they became fast friends.

Even on the days Lilly was not assigned to Erin, she would come from the other side of the hospital just to look in on her and do whatever she could to make Erin comfortable. And, as she said, it was when Lilly was on vacation that Erin coded.

Erin took a deep breath and shook her head. "Strange, very strange," she said.

"You made a lot of friends while you were up there, Erin." Jim's face, solemn. "So many of the employees would come by just to say hi and see how you were getting along. You were friendly to everyone. It's just who you are. You have that effect on people, Erin.   You're not going to believe this, but even the lady who did housekeeping in your room would offer to share her lunch with you. Whenever she saw that you didn't eat, she'd offer you her own food. I guess she thought you didn't like the hospital food and would prefer something homemade. Lilly would do the same. They would bring little treats and share them with you. You have no idea how much Lilly did for you."

A melancholy overwhelmed Erin because she couldn't make a warm connection with Lilly. How sad it had to be to care for someone so much and that someone to not remember you.

At that moment, she looked up at Jim and realized what he must be feeling. The heartbreak of knowing that his wife of so many years didn't want him to touch her. Not wanting his kisses or his embraces. Not recognizing his face, his touch, the sound of his voice, or the warmth of his breath on her skin.

And, yet, Jim continued to smile and to flirt with Erin. He remained at her side, day and night, never imposing his thoughts, words, or actions on her. At every opportunity, and even when there wasn't one, he always tried to make Erin laugh. His patience, and love, constantly displayed itself with ease and confidence.

Erin enjoyed his wit and humor. But, more than anything, Erin delighted in the gentle way he approached life. How he dealt with her life and all the insecurities that went along with it. No matter how difficult a situation was, he found a way to lighten the mood with a silly crack or a corny saying, each time more ridiculous and outrageous than the last. Had he always been this wonderfully funny? Or did he pretend all this just for her?

The answer didn't matter because the outcome was always the same. Around Jim, Erin continually felt the protective walls of her soul gently tumble down around her.

There was always Jim, patiently wearing his crooked little smile, sweeping up the pieces of her lost memories by explaining and/or expanding on a thought or a feeling she might experience. And, when there was no explanation, he would make up an improbable, senseless story to make her giggle. She could definitely feel something for this man. But, what that was, she hadn't figured out. His not allowing her to make any decisions about her daily routines or her health in general still sat like a rock in the pit of her stomach.

Betty

On a cold, cloudy Saturday morning, Erin stood in the doorway of the bathroom, looking out of the window at the rooftop of the neighbor's house.

"In or out, Grandma?" asked Sebastian.

"Out," Erin answered. "Bubba, what are all these bottles in the shower? I know about shampoo and conditioner. But, what's this body wash and why so many?"

"That's liquid soap for your body, Grandma. Mom and you use the Olay and Grandpa and I use the Old Spice."

"What's the difference between those and this bar of soap that I use?" Erin's confusion was evident on her face.

"I dunno! Smell, I guess. Oh, and Mom says it makes your skin soft. The one Gramps and I use makes us smell *manly*!"

"So many choices, it's confusing."

"If you're confused now, don't look in the medicine cabinet or under the sink. It'll really make you crazy! But, you'll have to do that a little later. 'Cause, I gotta go!"

"Oh, I'm sorry, Bubba." Erin stepped out of the bathroom, making a mental note to check those cupboards later.

And, so, she did. That same afternoon, she took everything out of the bathroom cupboard and began reading all the labels on the bottles of this and that. Cleaners, sparklers, softeners, scrubbers, and things to make the air smell... better. *That* she understood. There were three and four bottles or cans of one thing or another that seemed to do the exact same thing, only different! Why? She'd need to find out and eliminate some of the clutter.

Jim walked in and, horrified, asked, "What on Earth are you doing?" Immediately, he started picking up the mess that Erin had created, stating, "You don't need to be doing all this. You need to be resting. I'll take care of this!"

And, once again, he just took over. He didn't wait for her to answer his questions. Nor did he give her a chance to explain why she was looking and sorting through everything.

He took her by the arm and was about to escort Erin to the living room, when she stopped abruptly and said, "No! Wait! I was just wondering and reading what all that was and what it was for."

"You don't need ...

"Yes! Yes, I do need!" Erin's voice scaled up a few octaves. "I want to know. You say this is my house, so I need to be able to do things, and to know about things that everyone else does."

Jim's shocked face frightened Erin. But, she stood her ground. She didn't mean to hurt Jim, but she didn't know any other way to make him understand what she was feeling. So, there it was! Simple!

"I can do all this for you, and I can help you

figure all this out." Jim explained. "I just don't want you thinking you need to start cleaning and doing a bunch of housework. Understand?"

"Help, I can use," Erin replied. "What I can't use is you doing everything for me. Some things I can and would like to do for myself. I need to feel like I am part of this family, not an outsider being waited on all the time. Understand?"

They both stared into each other's eyes and out of nowhere, smiles and giggles erupted, flooding the small bathroom with laughter. What had started out to be a tense moment, ended with two people just learning a little about each other's character. It was that easy and, for Erin, it felt exhilarating!

Erin lay in the recliner, resting after her bath and dressing change, amazed at how simple cleanliness could be so uplifting, yet so exhausting. She was just about to doze off when she heard a woman clear her throat. Startled, her eyes popped open and was surprised to see Betty standing in front of her.

"Enjoying a lazy day, I see!" Betty's tone was sharp and insulting.

"Sorry, Betty. I didn't hear your knock."

"Knock? I never knock. Oh, I guess that's one of those things you conveniently don't remember," she said loudly. "I don't have to knock, 'cause I'm your sister!"

Elaine walked in and immediately spoke up, "Hi, Aunt Betty. I don't mean to be rude, but would you lower your voice a little? Mom lost her memory, not her hearing. She was just resting, she's had a busy morning and it's tired her out."

"You watch your tone, young lady! And you... what did you do," Betty sarcastically inquired. "Run a marathon?" Betty laughed, but her laughter wasn't amusing. "I'm kidding. I know you have a big hole in your belly. How's it doing? Is it beginning to shrink?"

"It's too early to tell, Auntie," Elaine answered, fuming at her aunt's insulting attitude. "The doctor said it would take months to heal."

"Lucky you," Betty sniped as she glared at Erin. "Your vacation is extended. Months even! No housework or cooking for you. And, you *love* doing that kind of stuff."

"I do?" asked Erin, looking to Elaine. "Dolly, can I cook?"

"Boy, can you cook, Mom!" responded Elaine. "But, I don't know that you necessarily like cooking and cleaning. I don't think you even stop to think about it. It needs to be done, so you just do it. That's just you, Mom."

"Well, I'm tired just thinking about it today!" retorted Erin, sighing deeply and closing her eyes momentarily.

Betty reached for the remote and changed the channel, making herself at home. She didn't ask, she just clicked on her favorite program and plopped herself down comfortably on the sofa.

"Aunt Betty," interrupted Elaine, "Mom was just about to watch 'Willy Wonka and the Chocolate Factory."

"Oh, that's a kid's movie," scolded Betty. "My soap opera is on. Do you mind?" She didn't wait for an answer; she just made herself cozy.

Suddenly, she jumped up and said, "I'm going to get something to drink, before I settle in. Do you want anything, water, soda, cookies?"

Erin looked at Elaine, questioning the situation with her eyes. Elaine shrugged her shoulders, "That's your sister!" was the only thing she whispered.

"Auntie, if you're going to be here for a while, could you stay with Mom for a few minutes? I need to step out and get some heavy cream. I've got soup cooking in the crock pot, and I'll be needing to add it pretty soon. Dad should be home in a few minutes. He was just going to the Post Office."

"Is that for dinner tonight? Mike will be coming over after work to visit, and he's not too keen on soup."

"I'm sorry, Auntie. But, cream of potato soup is what's on the menu, tonight. It's Mom's favorite and I'm hoping it'll trigger a memory. You're welcome to make Uncle Mike a bologna sandwich. We've got plenty of that in the fridge."

"Oh, no thanks. He doesn't like bologna. He likes a full dinner in the evening. No worries. I'm sure I can find something in the cupboards or the fridge for him to eat."

Erin kept her eyes shut tight. Afraid if she opened them, her mouth would also open and something terrible would fly out. Who was this person and why did she carry on so? Was this normal? Was it customary to walk in and out of people's homes and just take over? Erin wasn't sure, but it sounded rude and imposing. At the moment, Erin didn't consider it her place to say anything. At least, not yet.

She wasn't up to entertaining company, but Erin wasn't given a choice. It was clear that Betty had made plans with her husband to spend the afternoon and evening, including dinner, with Erin and her family. Betty's plans appeared to include relaxing, watching TV and eating.

"Don't be gone too long, Elaine." Betty ordered. "I don't want to be responsible if anything happens to your mom. Have you fed her yet? I'm kinda hungry myself. What's for lunch?"

"I'm right here, and nothing is going to happen to me that I can't handle." Annoyed at Betty's attitude, Erin promptly spoke up.

Elaine quickly walked back in the room, and the look on her face said a million nasty things. But, she held her composure, as well as her tongue, and no one would have known that she was miffed.

"Aunt Betty, I was about to give mom a chicken salad sandwich and some grapes. Would you like some?"

"Sure, you can fix me a sandwich, too. I love your mom's chicken salad," she answered.

"It's not Mom's, I made it. We're not letting mom in the kitchen yet. Doctor said she's to take it easy until her wound heals, and that won't be for a few months yet. Besides, she tires easily. On top of that, with an open wound, the kitchen isn't the best place for her. You know, with the infection and such."

Elaine retrieved the plate for Erin and, as she placed the food on the T.V. tray in front of Erin, she nonchalantly stated," You're welcome to help yourself, though. The sandwich bread is in the cupboard. But, you already know where everything is. Just make yourself at home." And quietly, under her breath but, within earshot of Erin she whispered, "Not that you don't always do that anyway!"

Erin snickered.

Betty was already in the kitchen grumbling something about having to fix her own sandwich. "You'd think that since I am the aunt and I'm in *her* house, she would have the decency and enough respect to *serve* me my lunch like she does her mother. What is wrong with this generation? If I had raised her, she wouldn't be so flippant and disrespectful."

"Will you be okay with her for a little bit, Mom?" asked Elaine, gritting her teeth. "I won't be long, I'm just going around the corner to the supermarket. And, Dad will be here any minute."

"I'll be fine. But, I don't promise *she'll* be the same person when you get back. Of that, you can be sure." Erin winked at her worried daughter, and the smirk on her face gave Elaine a peaceful feeling as she sighed and walked out the door. Erin, comfortable with the situation, just smiled.

"Betty, can I ask you a question?" The smirk still fresh on Erin's face.

"Yeah, sure," she said, sashaying back into the living room with her large sandwich and a plate piled high with a variety of chips. "What do ya wanna know?" A look of superiority covered Betty's face and the tone in her voice confirmed a slight high and mighty attitude.

"I ask because, well... you know, I don't remember. Anyway, I just want to know about how we get along as sisters. What is our relationship like? Is it okay to ask?" Erin had a plan, and, with a little luck, she would make her point gently, yet firmly.

"Yeah," Betty answered nastily. "I said okay, didn't I? So, just ask already!"

"I guess you come over here, often, right? Do I visit you, at your home I mean?" Erin looked straight at Betty.

"Not often. But, sometimes, why?" Betty's tone a bit softer.

"We're sisters, right? So... my question is... do I walk into your house without knocking, too? And, then, do I feel right at home in your house? Do you cook for me and for my family? I mean, is it the same at your house?" Erin smiled sweetly at Betty.

"Nooo...," she replied, her tone uncomfortable and guarded. "But, then, I'm really busy all the time." Betty felt a definite curve to the conversation. "So, you know you have to call me ahead of time, 'cause I might not be home or might be on my way out somewhere. Where are you going with this? Are you mad because I came over to check on your health? And, because my husband and I wanted to spend a little time with you?"

Sarcastically, Erin answered, "No, why would you think that! I'm just trying to learn about how sisterly love works. So, if I understand correctly, it's okay for you to come over, walk right in, make yourself at home, expect to stay for dinner, your family included, complain about the menu and treat my daughter badly. But, it's not okay for me to do the same? Is that right?" Erin couldn't believe all of that had spewed out of her mouth.

"Well, somebody's in a bad mood," Betty snapped. "You're being rude and mean to me! I know when I'm not appreciated. Here I am, taking time out of my busy schedule to … "

"No, no, no," Erin softly interrupted. "Since I can't remember, I just want to figure out how things work between us. You know, the comfort level between us sisters. That's all."

"Why are you treating me like this? Like I'm a nobody?" grumbled Betty. "What's happened to you? You were never like this before. My family and I have always been welcomed in your home, any day and any time. You always said your home was my home. I practically raised my girls in this house and now your acting like I'm an acquaintance, not your sister. What is wrong with you? Did something happen to change your heart when it stopped? I don't think I like your attitude now. Never mind about lunch or dinner. I deeply apologize if I was imposing." She plopped her plate on the coffee table in front of Erin.

"I'll come back when you're in a better mood. If I come back, at all!" Betty grabbed her sweater and her purse and stomped out of the door. "And, by the way," she said, sneering back at Erin, "you're not fooling me, sister. I know you're just pretending not to remember things. I don't know why, but if it works for you, then more power to ya. But your game is up with me. I know you. You... malingerer!"

Erin took a deep breath, and the smirk became an accomplished smile. Her point had been made and the snotty, spoiled, little sister had been put in her place. Erin didn't know how things worked before, but they were definitely in for a change.

On the other hand, losing another person in her already-empty life didn't sit well in her heart. Another battle had begun. Where it would end up would be interesting.

The Letter

Erin comfortably ate her lunch, then took the opportunity to explore a few more areas in the house. She opened a small drawer in the computer desk and fumbled through some old paid bills. A ledger, pens, pencils, paper clips, and a few old letters cluttered the tiny space.

There were a few long business envelopes addressed to Ms. Erin Berger with some of the most beautiful paintings of a Geisha covering the entire back of the stationary. Erin didn't recognize the name of the sender, so after admiring the incredible artwork, she put the letters back. There was one envelope addressed to "Mom", so thinking it was for her, Erin opened the correspondence.

It read:

May 13, 1990

Dear Mom:

Last night I was cleaning out my purse and found a whole lot of small pieces of paper in a compartment of my wallet. They were I.O.U.'s and guess who they were all made out to? Yes, you guessed it. They're all made out to you.

I owe you so much in my life that this is just one tiny drop in an ocean of debt so huge, there wouldn't be enough trees for the amount of paper I would need to write it all down. Here are just a few that come to mind.

I owe you for being a night nurse. For staying up all those nights when I was sick as a child as well as when I wasn't sick and just needed for you to hold me while I fell asleep.

I owe you for being a night watchman and staying up, worrying while I was out late on a date. Then, quietly slipping up to bed before I walked in the house, so I wouldn't think you were spying.

In addition, for all the nights you did not sleep because you were up praying for me when I no longer lived in your house but continued to occupy your heart.

I owe you for much needed medical advice, like don't be kissing the boys because you'll get some infectious disease.

For just being my mom and kissing my scrapes, then assuring me that I would heal. Or, for telling me I would get better at whatever I was trying to accomplish, when my pride was aching because I thought I was a failure at some small task that was monumental to me.

For telling me that my heart would heal when it was broken. And, of course, for when you told me to make sure I always wore clean underwear, just in case I was in an accident and needed to go to the hospital. It sounds silly now, but the advice was so important.

I owe you for being a veterinarian, feeding and taking care of our dogs, rabbits, chickens, *roosters (which I hated), and for curing puppy love.*

I owe you for making hamburger taste like steak, making banana splits with blackberry syrup that you had made from the blackberry bushes in the back yard. And, on hot summer days, for making bologna sandwiches and serving them with a pitcher of "Sonny Boy" lime syrup and cracked ice, instead of soda.

I owe you for making the prettiest 'Cut up' cakes for our Bake Sales, out of the few pieces of cake that Dad didn't eat. And especially for managing to form that beautiful swan out of the last, few pieces of cake that he left sitting in the pan.

For the times that I would get a taste in my mouth of life being unfair, you were always there to give me one of your home-baked pastries with a hug and a kiss. For restoring the sweet taste of a mother's love and giving me the courage and confidence to go on when all I wanted to do was quit whatever was beating me down.

I owe you for being a seamstress and a tailor. For the times when there was very little money and you took an inexpensive piece of cloth that you purchased at the local yardage store and created a spectacular dress that made me look like a model stepping out of a magazine.

I owe you for the taxi service you provided all those times you carried me, my dates, and my friends to parties and dances. Were it not for you, none of us would have gone anywhere. For taking me to the doctor, the dentist, school, work, shopping and just for a ride when I needed to talk.

I owe you for being my best friend and for understanding when no one else would, and for setting me straight when I needed mental grounding. For all the advice you gave me as a child and I now give to my own. For the scoldings you gave because you loved me and did not want me to go through the same hurts you had experienced throughout your life. And, now, I give those same scoldings because I love and want to protect my child.

I owe you for being a banker, a grocer, a counselor, a doctor, and just for being my mom. When times were lean, and my family had nothing to eat, you filled my cupboards and fed us, never asking for anything in return except to know that our stomachs were full.

I know that in my lifetime I will never, ever be able to repay all that I owe you. And, I know that you would say that all would be repaid with a hug and a kiss and those three little words, "I love you".

So, collect your hugs and your kisses now. For that is all that I have to give. And, as you have said so many times, "Hugs and kisses are free, but so very valuable!" And, know, that from the depths of my heart and the center of my soul, 'I love you', Mom!

Signed,
Erin

In that moment, Erin realized that the letter had not been written for her, but by her and addressed to her own mother, who was no longer of this world.

In a flash, she remembered the face in the photographs. Her heart ached, and tears rushed down her face. She remembered a tough, strong woman standing in front of an old stove, making tortillas and the tantalizing smell that rose from each one. The recollection of a little girl, standing, waiting patiently for the first one off the griddle, hot, soft and smeared with just a small pat of butter. Erin's mouth watered at the thought of taking that first bite of love-filled deliciousness.

It was a full memory, and it was Erin's. She let the tears fall and the memory engulf her, warm and reassuring. Her hands holding the letter to her breast, as if it would open up the flood gates allowing the pouring in of faces and names and places and things that were currently eluding her. Hoping and wishing all the memories would be as vivid.

But, it was only one. Endearing, heartfelt and private, just for Erin. A memory so precious that the clouds in her eyes gave way to a storm of tears and emotions. All the nothingness in her present and her past came pouring out of her soul. She had found one, solitary memory and it was a starting point. She could build her life from here.

Perhaps she would never remember any more of her former life. But, for now, Erin knew who she came from. Who she belonged to. Remembering what she looked like as a child, the smells of her mother's kitchen and the taste of homemade love, in the form of a fresh, buttered, flour tortilla.

Jim walked in the door, and Elaine followed behind. "Look who I found in the driveway." Jim's face was beaming.

"Who found who, Dad?" Giggling, Elaine poked her dad in the ribs. One look at Erin's tear streaked face, and Jim's laugh disappeared. "What's wrong? Why are you crying? Are you in pain?" Frightened that he had left Erin for too long and she was hurt, he rushed over to her chair and knelt beside her. "Tell me! What is it?"

"Mom?" Elaine was at her side. "How can I help?"

"I'm fine, I'm okay," Erin's trembling voice was a soft hush. "I've remembered something. My mother making tortillas. I remember her face and her scent and the warmth of her hugs. And, I remember her kitchen and the smell and taste of her cooking."

Slowly, she pulled the letter from her breast and handed it to Jim. "I found this in the desk drawer. I thought it was addressed to me. But I wrote this letter to my mother. And, after I read it, this wonderful memory surfaced and hugged me."

"It's a start," whispered Jim. "A great start."

A German Christmas

The days progressed slowly, and no more memories graced Erin. The depression once again threatened to engulf her.

Elaine suggested that she go through some old photo albums. But, after a few pages, Erin refused to sit and sift through picture after picture of people and places she didn't recognize. About to give up, she tossed the album aside, and it fell open to a page that provoked Erin to take a second look.

It was a photograph of Erin and Jim, at a very early age, standing in front of a castle, just beyond a river. A large baby bump around Erin's middle section brought a smile on her face and a warm, cozy feeling in her heart. She didn't remember when or where she was. But, it was an immense satisfaction knowing it had been a happy time in their life together. Gently, she closed the picture album.

She put her head back and closed her eyes.

"Just pick up the tip of the tree, and I'll take up the slack as I carry the trunk." Jim was beaming, and Erin couldn't control her giggles. She was laughing so hard, she couldn't stand up straight.

"How will we get it up the hill and then up the stairs?" she asked her soldier husband, breathless. *"It's so big and full, the decorations are going to get lost. We only have one string of lights and twelve*

Christmas balls." Again, the giggles overtook her, and she folded over, laughing hysterically.

"Come on, help me! Or, Christmas Eve will find us right here at the bottom of the hill, with no lights at all." Laughing uncontrollably, Jim struggled to take charge of the situation. It's a good thing you speak the lingo," Jim added. "Those Germans were trying to scalp me. They wanted thirteen marks for this monster of a tree. You walk around to the other side of the lot without me and talk to them and immediately the price drops to six marks. What did you say to them?"

"That the G.I. who wanted the tree was an idiot. In perfect German, I might add! They thought I was one of them, so they gave it to me at the local's price. Pretty good, huh?" Erin's words were barely audible for the chuckle. So much so, she was snorting.

She opened her eyes and reached for the album

"Jim, where was this?" Erin's thoughts whirling around in disorder as she sifted through more pictures of soldiers and castles and what looked like a military base.

"That's Budingen, Germany," Jim answered, a crooked smile covering his face. "I was stationed there for two years with the Army. It was right after we were married. What a lucky bride you were. No ordinary honeymoon for you. No, Ma'am. I took you to Europe for two years. Stephen was born there."

"He's German?" she asked.

"Actually," replied Jim. "He had dual citizenship until he was eighteen. After that, the United States no longer recognized the German, and he kept his American Citizenship. I don't know how it is today. But, when we were there, babies of military personnel, born abroad, were given citizenship through the parent. In our case, I swore the oath for Stephen. That's how they issued his citizenship and his passport, so he could travel back to the United States. Without that, he would have had to stay there."

Erin recounted her memory, and Jim gladly explained that the large tree she remembered was the first Christmas tree of their married life. He laughed loudly as he remembered the love they shared. Erin's smile lit up her face. All she recalled was a huge tree with one short string of lights and twelve small, yet beautiful Christmas bulbs. But it was enough. She knew they had been extremely happy.

Another snippet of information and another piece to add to the puzzle but, still, no complete picture. Yet, she was grateful. Little by little, Erin would piece together some of her past and attach it to her present.

Graduation

Erin slid onto the examining table with Jim's help and gingerly lay down. Jim didn't wait for the nurse to attend to Erin. He automatically began to remove her bandages and packing with the skill and proficiency of a seasoned professional. The staff all knew he was more than capable and were grateful for his help.

"Hi, how are you two doing?" Dr. Cabral cheerfully addressed the two as she stepped up and hugged Erin. "How are you, mama?" Donning the latex gloves, she examined Erin's wound.

"I'm good." answered Erin. Seeing Dr. Cabral was the highlight of her week. She so looked forward to her visits to see and speak with the beautiful doctor who saved her life. No matter how badly she was feeling, seeing Dr. Cabral at the clinic made her physically and mentally feel better. Each week, she was stronger, healthier and her deep wound was closing nicely.

"You're doing great, mama," Dr. Cabral stated. "By the way, I want to make a date with you. When you are completely healed and feeling totally well, we need to get together and share a meal to celebrate. What do you think?"

"Sounds like a good plan," Erin answered with a smile bigger than a slice of cantaloupe. "I'll work hard on getting there, Doctor."

Erin was so was grateful for all the care, but, mostly, Erin was extremely thankful for the kindness and patience Sara always shared. Perhaps she was this way with all her patients, and, from what Erin had heard, that was a fact. Dr. Sara Cabral treated and cared for each and every patient as if, at that moment, no others existed. Her patients loved and respected her for the dignity and respect she showed them. It didn't matter how badly she was feeling, physically, or how alone she felt in her mental chaos, talking to Dr. Cabral always centered her and grounded her emotions.

"The pain isn't as bad anymore. It's still there, but every day, it's better. What do you think, is it healing?"

"Yes, I'd say it's doing very well." Dr. Cabral turned to Jim. "You're doing a great job, Jim. I think you can decrease the dressing changes to twice a day now. And, instead of coming in every other day, once a week will be fine. And," she said, turning to Erin, "you've graduated. You can get in the shower now. Take the dressings off and just let the soap and water run over everything. Don't wash or scrub the wound. When you get out, Jim should irrigate it again and pack it, as usual. How's your appetite? Are you eating okay?"

"Like I said, I'm good. And, I'll be so much better now that I can shower." Elated, Erin reached for Dr. Cabral's arm. "Thank you, doctor."

"Call me 'Sara'," she said. "I think after all we've been through together, we should be on a first name basis. Don't you? How's your memory? Anything significant?"

"A few breakthroughs." Erin's face went dark and pensive as she filled the doctor in. "It's slow, but I have hope."

"Don't give up, mama! When you get down and depressed, try to remember that you could be in a worse state. Not only mentally, but physically as well. I know it's easy for me to say that, but, for everything your body has gone through, you're fortunate to be having this conversation. Some patients never recover enough to do even that. Hang in there."

Again, Sara Cabral hugged her patient, turned to Jim and said, "Can you handle this?" pointing to Erin's stomach. "Here are all the supplies you need. Or, do you prefer to have one of the nurses do it?"

"No," said Jim. "I've got this, doc... Sara." Erin reached out and caught Dr. Cabral's elbow.

"Doctor... Sara, I'll never be able to repay what you've done for me... for what I feel, here in my heart."

"And," replied Sara, "I'll never be able to repay you for what you've done for me. You don't understand how all this has impacted my life. Prior to finding you unresponsive, I was a lowly intern. A nothing, pondering my place in this hospital, on this Earth. I questioned whether I had made the right choice, going back to school to become a doctor. Because of you and what we've experienced together, I am now looked at and treated differently.

I'm no longer *just* an intern. I am now given the respect of a physician. And, I know this is where I want to be, doing what I want to do for the rest of my life: helping people survive illness and get on with life. Perhaps making it better than what it was before I got involved. And … it is I who am grateful to the universe for putting you in *my* path." Erin Berger and Sara Cabral had already bonded. But, at that specific moment, the alliance tightened.

"You know that this bond is forever," said Erin, her eyes filled with tears from her healing heart.

"Yes, for as long as we live," Dr. Cabral confirmed, her own tears gracing her beautiful face.

"Well," said Erin, with a tired smile. "I hope that, if the time comes that I'm ready to die, you're right there to cheat death and save me one more time!"

The two women hugged. "I'll do what I can, if I can," replied Sara.

Jim, feeling like he was walking on sunshine, made the appointment for the following week. Week after week, month after month, the appointments with Sara Cabral continued, as Erin's wounds healed, her health improved, and an even closer friendship developed.

On one occasion, as Erin and Jim walked out of the clinic after Erin's appointment with Dr. Cabral, Annie, the EKG Technician bumped into them.

"Mrs. Berger," she sheepishly spoke. Her eyes lowered, barely looking at Erin.

"Annie, how nice to see you again. How are

you? Is everything going okay for you?" Concerned, Erin questioned the timid employee.

"I'm doing well, thank you for asking." The shy hospital worker reached out and took Erin's hand and firmly squeezed it.

"Thank you, Mrs. Berger," she whispered, and took her leave.

Erin never knew what it was all about. Only that this young woman felt at peace when she touched her hand. And, that was fine with Erin.

Dreaming on a jet plane

Erin sat in the tattered, blue recliner, staring out of the living room window. The roaring blare of a jet engine filled the house as it flew overhead towards the airport, causing the house to rattle. She closed her eyes and drifted off with the humming of the engines still in the air. Erin's heart was in that jet, on her way to a land far away.

She had never traveled by herself before. Yet, on this hot and sticky night of August, in the year 1969, here she was, on board an airplane traveling across the United States and ready to cross the Atlantic Ocean. Her destination, Frankfurt, Germany. Was anyone going to be there to meet her? She didn't know. But, that didn't put a damper on her plans. She was prepared to face whatever circumstances stood before her, even if it meant she would find herself in a strange country, with no one to depend on and no one to lean on. In eighteen hours, she would know if this journey would prove to be an adventure or a nightmare.

Like so many young women of the late 1960's, Erin Nava had fallen in love with a soldier. Although Jim wasn't a soldier when they first met, and just when everything was going so smoothly in their relationship, the draft saw to it that their hearts would be pulled apart. While plans were being made for a traditional wedding in April and arrangements were being finalized for the church, hall, caterer, orchestra and wedding invites were being ordered, Jim received his draft notice.

In late March of 1969, he was drafted into the United States Army and shipped off to Fort Ord in Northern California. When and if he would return to be married was not talked about or even considered. Soldiers belonged to the government, not to their girlfriends or family. All plans were temporarily postponed with no future date in view.

It was the height of the Vietnam war, and young men were returning home in body bags. Those that were lucky enough to make it home alive were not always in one piece. Consequently, against Erin's wishes and love-encased judgment, her family interceded and insisted that waiting would be the best thing to do.

With Jim in boot camp, she was unable to communicate with her soulmate, the love of her life and greatest ally, to discuss further plans. She was alone, facing the cancellations, family member opinions and harsh remarks from the family elders with an ache in her heart that refused to be silenced.

In addition, there were eight bridesmaids who had paid good money to have their dresses made and shoes dyed to match, just for the privilege of being in the wedding party. Those long-time friends and relatives, who were so happy and excited and begging to be part of the nuptials, were now asking, and some demanding, reimbursement for said dresses and accessories. Never considering the word, 'postponement', everyone was writing the whole thing off, as if Jim had already been killed, never to return.

"This is war, something you don't understand," bellowed her Uncle Max. He was Erin's mother's brother and had fought during War World II. He served one tour of four years in the Navy and two tours, four years each, in the Army. He often stated that he should have stayed in the military and retired from his service. Unknown to him, his family agreed.

"You need to wait until he finishes his tour of duty and then get married. What if he doesn't return? And, if he does get back, are you so sure you'll still want to marry him, if he only has one leg or one arm or worse, none at all? You're being stupid making all these plans. Typical female! Always thinking about romance and frilly dresses. Because of all this nonsense, now you're stuck having to pay for all this wedding foolishness."

Uncle Max was a bachelor by choice and didn't think much of a woman's point of view. To him, it was a man's world, logical and stable. Common sense was the only thing that mattered in life and, in his mind, men moved the world and women stayed home, ran the house and the kids, and had no say in worldly matters.

Having no children of his own, he considered his sister's children much like his own. Unfortunately, his sisters all looked up to him and valued his opinions much more than those of their own husbands. He was well educated, mostly due to his love of books, and extremely knowledgeable and well-traveled through the military. In the family circle, his was always the last word to consider. Consequently, whatever he advised was looked upon as the family law.

His heart was in the right place, wanting to protect the family, but his opinions were not always gentle, and very seldom solicited, yet always accepted as final.

But, not today. For the first time in the family history, someone was going to stand up to him and that someone was Erin.

Weighing her words carefully, for she wanted him to hear everything she had to say, but she didn't want to offend or disrespect her uncle, she spoke with determination. Erin loved him, but she wasn't a little girl anymore. She was in love and nothing or no one would be allowed to come between her and her love.

She stood up from the dining room table, looked Uncle Max straight in the eyes, and, with all the courage she could muster together, she released the words from her heart:

"It is not foolishness, Uncle Max. We love each other," Erin's voice was soft yet firm. "I'm not in love with his arms or his legs, I'm in love with his heart and soul and the person that he is. And, even if we get married and it only lasts one day because something terrible happens to him and he never returns, we would have had that one day together as husband and wife. We would complete each other for that one day. And, if destiny dictates that he comes back with only one arm or half a body, I will love him and care for him until I have no breath left in mine. I don't care about a big wedding, but I do care about being his wife for however long it's meant."

"You think you're so smart because you're a nurse and make some big money," he barked. "You think you're smarter than all of us who have lived life and know what it is to make it out in the world, scraping to make a living. We know what's best for you, if you'll only listen.

"If you're so smart, then why are you still living here with your parents. They support you and give you security. You've got it made here, so it's easy to make stupid decisions, while riding on their ticket. If you were living out there on your own, you wouldn't be so quick to spend all your money on the luxuries of one wedding day. If anything happens to that man of yours, you are here, with your parents picking up the slack for your flippant decisions. You have no worries."

"First of all," stated Erin. Her voice a little louder than before but, still in control. "I live here because our culture dictates that I do so until I am married. Second, Jim and I are paying for this wedding, mistakes and all. I haven't and will not ask for any help from anyone in this family. You and the rest of this family have decided to make it your business and to impose your opinions as to what I should or should not do. No one has asked what Jim or I want or are thinking. As usual, it has been decided for me. WRONG! The decision to marry, now or later, is still ours and for now, while he is away, I will decide what is best.

"My parents have given me their permission to marry Jim. You, yourself, said he was the best man I could marry. You've worked with him and know the kind of man he is. So, please stop interfering. Just   let us be happy and go on with our plans."

At that moment, not a breath was heard. Erin looked at her parents. Her mother's eyes were looking down at her hands, and her father was sitting at the head of the table with his shoulders slumped and his eyes wide in disbelief.

"I'm sorry for disrespecting your house, Daddy," her eyes implored his understanding. "But, I'm not sorry for what I have said. I love all of you and understand your concern for my future. And, if leaving this house and proving myself to all of you is what I need to do, then so be it. But, whatever I do, it will be what I think is best for me. And, whether the family approves or disapproves is of no consequence to me anymore." Erin moved away from the table, and, without looking back, walked to her room, sat on her bed and stared out of the window into the back yard.

For the first time in her life, her fathers' beautiful gardens gave her no comfort. She felt the suppressed, lonely child in her soul no longer. The woman inside her had stood up and was pushing to come out and sing. There were no tears, no ache in her heart. She took a deep breath and felt a weight *had been lifted from her soul. No longer was she the little girl trying to be an adult. She was a grown woman, feeling ten feet tall.*

Erin had finished nursing school with honors and conquered her state boards. She had worked in the Emergency Room at the largest hospital in the city and now worked in the operating room, standing side by side with surgeons and literally had patient's lives in the palm of her hands. And yet, her family didn't believe she should make any decisions regarding her own life. How could it be that complete strangers trusted their lives in her hands, yet her own family didn't think she had the capability to make her own life work?

Was it because she was the first woman in the family to get an education, or was it that she was a Mexican-American female and culture dictated that she allow the males in the family to run all that they thought was important? Erin knew her place but refused to stay there. She was choosing a mate that respected her thoughts and point of view, never treating her submissively. She was his equal, in every circumstance. Now, in his absence, they were taking advantage of her situation and trying to put a stop to all their dreams and plans.

At the moment, she had no choice and all plans were canceled. But, it was only a temporary situation.

Approximately two weeks later, a letter arrived from Jim, and communication began on a regular basis. Erin was back to being her old self again. She continued working, and the only plan made was to travel up north to his graduation from boot camp. Jim would be given a pass for a three-day leave. He would have to return to the base and report in each evening by nine. But, the days would be free to do as he pleased.

Not thinking she would be accompanied, plans were made to spend the entire time together, alone. But, Erin's mother got wind of it, and made it clear that she would make the trip with her. Unmarried Hispanic young women of her age and culture didn't just take off and spend a weekend alone with a man, no matter how engaged she happened to be. Erin's brother and Jim's brother and sister would also make the trip. It wasn't the reunion they would have liked, but it didn't matter. She and Jim would be together. And, when they were together, no one else existed.

After the graduation ceremonies, Jim informed them that his orders were to leave for his Advanced Infantry Training in Fort Sill, Oklahoma, in two days. The talk on the base was that after their A.I.T. of two months, they would get some time off on leave before the entire unit would be shipped to Vietnam. But, as always in the military, unless it was written in your orders, it wasn't confirmed. Jim could be sent anywhere, at any time and for any length of time. He would just have to wait and see. Wedding plans again were postponed for an undetermined amount of time.

Erin and Jim would have to make the best of

the two days they had. And, they made sure their time was spent with their bodies as close as possible. With no privacy, their words were spoken in whispers, and their eyes melted into each other's like pools of rippling want, with each and every glance. They agreed to wait until Jim's training was over to make any definite plans. At that time, he would know exactly where his orders would send him and for how long.

The rumor on the graduation field was that he would get three weeks of leave. But, that rumor had been spread about the time they would get off after Boot Camp and three weeks turned out to be two days. It was wartime, and nothing was concrete. Orders were being changed from one day to the next and from moment to moment. How long of a leave, if any and where he would end up, was anyone's guess. The only thing that Jim and Erin knew for sure was that at the first chance possible, they would be married, if only by the Justice of the Peace.

The group spent one day visiting Jim's uncle's strawberry farm close to the base. They picked and ate berries until their lips and fingers were stained a deep, reddish purple and their stomachs ached. Laughing and feeling the love of family was beautiful but didn't erase the ache of wanting to be alone that Erin and Jim struggled to control.

The following day, they took the seventeen-mile drive along the coast of the Monterrey Peninsula and through the lovely seaside city of Carmel. Never had Erin observed so much of nature's beauty.

Perhaps it was the sea and the salty air, or maybe it was being so close to the love of her life that inspired her to breathe in his essence and tuck it away in a secret place, where only she and Jim could secretly visit.

There, standing in the wet sand, the salt water lapping at their feet, the two lovers, in a world all their own, could sense the pounding of the ocean in their trembling bodies. Each time the sea foam caressed the shore, Erin longed to kiss Jim and engulf his body with her own. But a public display of affection was not something that a decent young woman would allow herself, ever. Especially in front of her mother. So, the two held hands, tightly, sighed heavily in unison and let the water cool their passion.

At the end of the two days, their goodbye was swift and filled with pain and anxiety. Intimacy of any kind was totally out of the question. There was no sensual embrace or passionate kiss. Only the look of two lovers aching for each other's touch, their eyes saying all that was not verbalized through clouds of tears. The pain in their hearts as well as their quivering bodies was displayed on their two young faces for all present to witness.

"I love you," whispered Jim. "I'll write as soon as I'm settled, and I'll phone you if there's a phone booth anywhere near."

"I love you, too." Erin's voice was barely audible.

"Enough," Erin's mother announced. "He belongs to the government now, and he has a duty to his country, not to you." Abruptly, she stepped between the two lovers and separated them.

"Go on, now. You need to get back to your job of defending our country and our freedom. And, we need to get going back to L.A." She didn't mean to be gruff; It was just her way of ending a tense moment and keeping her daughter's thoughts chaste. She would not allow Erin to experience anything remotely physical, let alone sexual. At least, not until she was married. And, if she had anything to say about it, her daughter would not be getting married until Jim was discharged from the Army, two years down the road.

Erin watched as Jim walked slowly away from her arms and back to the barracks. Her eyes stayed glued to his image until he no longer could be seen.

It would be a long six hours back to Los Angeles and an even longer eight weeks until she would see her love again, her heart exploding with pain and longing, stifled her breathing, robbing her head of oxygen, her eyes overflowing with tears that refused to stay hidden. Slowly, she walked towards the car, refusing to look back for fear of giving in to the cry that was stuck in her throat.

Everyone in the car slept or just didn't feel the need to make conversation. The tension was thick as molasses on burnt toast and Erin's heart was sagging low in her chest as she drove south to Los Angeles without the warmth and support of the man she so loved. Facing more familial opinions and advice from relatives who had no business in her and Jim's business was on the upcoming weekend agenda.

Jim's advice to her was, "Just don't let them get to you. As soon as I know what the Army expects from me, I'll let you know and then we'll make our plans and follow through. No one can keep us apart. Whatever time we have, we'll spend it together. You can count on that, I promise. I'm never going to let you go, Erin."

Upon their arrival in L.A., as usual, the family was gathered to welcome them home and to hear all the gossip regarding Erin's plans. It was late, but they were all there, waiting. Uncle Max, Aunt Minnie and Uncle Jake, along with Erin's father, waited impatiently for the news of Jim's orders.

Jim's brother and sister took their leave, not wanting to be involved in Erin's expected family battle. Once again, opinions not wanted were given and orders were attempted to be enforced.

Erin was questioned, and when the answers she gave were disputed, she was accused of expecting a child. That, they implied, being the reason she wanted so badly to marry before Jim's tour of duty was over. Insulted, hurt and refusing to take the abuse any longer, Erin stood quietly and announced she was leaving home.

"I've had enough, and I need to prove to myself that I know what I'm doing is the right thing." Erin's voice was soft yet determined. "I don't need to prove anything to any of you. You're right, Uncle Max. I make more money than any of you and maybe I should be standing on my own two feet. Since what you say seems to be the law around here, then culture or no culture, I'm assuming that you approve of me leaving my parents' home and living on my own. So, as of this day, I'm out of here."

"No, Erin," said her dad. "You can't do this. You're tired from the trip and sad because Jim is going to 'Nam. Go to bed and get some rest. You'll feel better in the morning."

"I'm sorry, Dad," Erin sadly responded to her father, her heart breaking that he didn't say anything to defend her. "But, I need to do this." And she walked to her bedroom.

Betty had been listening and couldn't believe Erin was actually leaving home. She was protesting and crying.

"Don't leave, Erin. Don't leave me, please!" she cried. "Who's going to take care of me? You're the only one who listens to me and buys stuff for me. Stuff I really like. If you insist on leaving then, could you leave me some money? You know, so I can get by?"

Erin had always looked out for Betty, but she was determined to take her leave. She didn't think it was right that all Betty could think about was herself, but, not thinking clearly and worried she was leaving Betty to face the family alone, she gave Betty some money. Then, she proceeded to pack a few articles of clothing, her nurse's cap, uniform and shoes. Not wanting to confront the family again, Erin didn't walk out of the door. She stealthily climbed out of her bedroom window, quietly got in her car, drove off, and never looked back. She didn't know here she was going. She just kept driving, her tears constantly falling. Somehow, she ended up at her friend and co-worker's house.

When her friend, Corinne, opened the door, all she said was, "It's about time!"

That night and the following day, Erin tried desperately to contact Jim to no avail. Not even the Red Cross would get a message to him. Fiancées were not a priority during a war situation. She would have to wait for him to contact her. And, so she did.

The following day she contacted Jim's brother and immediately he told her to come to his house. His sister had a little back house that was empty, and it would be home to Erin as long as she needed it. He wanted to be sure that Jim would be able to find her when he called looking for her.

Erin protested but Jim's brother wouldn't hear it. "I promised Jim I'd make sure you were okay and that's just what I'm doing. You'd still be living on you own, but at least you'll be close by and we're all here if you need us."

Erin moved in, and Jim's younger sister moved in with her. She was a few years younger than Erin, but the two were already great friends. Since neither young woman had ever lived alone before, this was a comfortable situation.

As luck would have it, Erin just happened to be at Jim's older sister's house when he called looking for her. He had called Erin at home and all her mother told him was that she had run away from home and she didn't know or care where Erin was.

He was frantic and decided to call his family just in case Erin had contacted them and was relieved to hear her voice.

After much affirmation and a bit of arguing, Erin convinced Jim that she was well, and it was decided that Erin would continue to work until Jim finished his training and received his orders, before making any final plans.

"I'll send you some money," he told Erin.

"I don't need anything. I'm fine. I still have my job, so I don't need any money," she assured him.

"As soon as I know my orders, I'll call you," Jim continued. "No matter where they deploy me, we'll be married before I go. I've already put all my papers in order with your name as beneficiary. Erin, stay there with my sisters."

"There's a little two-bedroom house for rent on their same street, Jim, and your sister Fran and I are going to move in. We're already living together here. I'm fine, quit worrying. Just let me know where you're going and when you're coming home."

Betty Remembers

Erin woke with a jolt to the sound of the knock on the door.

"Grandma, open the door, I forgot my key," Sebastian cried urgently, his voice loud and high pitched.

"Coming," she answered. "I know, I know. You're in a hurry to use the bathroom."

Frantically, Sebastian touched Erin's arm and blew her a kiss, as he ran past her.

"Gee, I love that boy!" Her heart had learned how warm and wonderful it was to be a grandmother. Every day, he astounded her with his bright smile and his knowledge of so many things, things he was willing to share and teach her about their life together and about current events and school shenanigans. He also taught her about the computer, something that had enchanted Erin. He was a wonder, full of wit and energy. Constantly, surprising her and making her laugh at the smallest things. He was a lot like Jim in his character, and that was a good thing.

She sat in her chair and wondered at the memory she had just experienced. Or, was it a dream full of crazy thoughts? Who were all those people. She knew their names and even what some of them looked like. Erin felt the hurt in her heart and the anguish in her soul. Did it all happen? Jim would answer her questions. He would know, and soon, she would place another piece of the puzzle.

It wasn't Jim who answered Erin's questions that day. As she was waiting for Jim to come in from working in the garage, Betty walked up the stairs and knocked heavily on the front door.

"Do I have permission to come in or do I need an appointment?" Sarcastically, Betty shouted.

"It's open, come on in," Erin responded. "How are you, Sis?"

"Not as good as you, but I manage." Her tone strained, Betty was trying, but it was evident that she still harbored ill feelings toward Erin. "How's the hole in your belly?" she inquired. She didn't hug or kiss Erin. She didn't even attempt to sit. She just stood over her, looking down with a superior stance.

"Relax, Betty. Sit down. Would you like something to drink?" Betty rolled her eyes, but Erin's invitation was accepted happily.

"Don't bother, I can get it myself," Betty answered as she walked into the kitchen and opened the fridge.

Some things hadn't changed, but it was obvious that Erin had made an impression on her sister. Her attitude was still a bit uppity, but her actions were not as imposing. For how long was anyone's guess.

Betty walked over and was getting ready to settle herself on the sofa when Erin approached her. "Betty, can I ask you something?"

"Oh, so now you want my opinion on

something, huh?" her words sharp and cutting.

"No, not really," patiently, Erin answered. "I just have a question. But, if you don't want to do this ..."

"Okay, okay! Ask me..." Betty scrunched her face and, plopped herself down in front of Erin, waiting impatiently.

"How and where did Jim and I get married?"

"You selfishly eloped!" snapped Betty. "You had this big, fancy wedding planned and made everybody spend all this money to get dresses and shoes and everything. Mom already had your wedding dress practically finished. Then, you got into a big nasty fight with the family and left home. I tried to get you to stay, but you had made up your mind, so you climbed out the window and just took off. Leaving me alone, crying and scared."

"So, what happened?" Agitated, Erin's patience was all but gone.

"Nothing," replied Betty. "About two months later, you showed up with Jim and announced that you were going to Texas to get married, 'cause he wasn't twenty-one yet and needed his dad's signature for the marriage license. And, that his orders were sending him to Germany, not 'Nam, and you were going with him. Period. You weren't asking permission, you were making a statement. You invited Mom and Dad to go to Texas, but, of course, they said no. Why would they? After all, you had run away. And, that was that. You took off and, when you got back two weeks later, you were married and just had enough time to pack up and take the plane to Germany."

"I went by myself?" Erin asked in disbelief, pondering her dream or memory or whatever it was.

"Yup, nobody knew how you were going to do it. We didn't even know if you had any money. But, stubbornly, off you went."

"I guess I managed. I just had what I guess was a memory of something like that."

"Oh, come on, Erin. Stop with the charade. You don't have to pretend with me. The lies have to stop sometime." Betty's left eyebrow was up in the air, her smile off to one side. At this point in the conversation, she abruptly stood up, and standing with one hand on her hip, her stance defied Erin to deny the accusation.

Erin looked up and shook her head, grateful for what she had learned, although disgusted at her sister's malicious thoughts. "Think what you will, Betty. I'm not going to try and convince you of anything. I'm alone in this nightmare. You don't have to be a part of it. I appreciate the information you've given me today and seriously wish we could come to some form of peace between us. But, from the looks of things, you don't trust me anymore than I believe I can trust you. And, I'm sorry for that. It's too bad we can't be friends. I guess, maybe, it's my loss since I don't remember having any other friends."

"Oh, you have friends, lots of them. Jim's just been keeping them away. You've already seen some of them at the hospital, remember? Or are you pretending you've forgotten that, too?"

"Betty," Erin asked. "Why are you so angry with me? What did I do to you to make you so hostile towards me? Did I hurt you in some way? What is it?"

"I'm not angry," Betty retorted. "It's you, always you. You're the one that knows everything and does everything right. Now, you've figured out a way to get more attention and just lay around and be waited on, hand and foot. As if Jim doesn't do everything for you already. Give him a break, Erin. Stop using him as your personal servant."

At that moment, Sebastian walked in the room, behind Betty. She didn't see him, but she followed Erin's glance over her shoulder, towards the door. Immediately, her tone and attitude changed.

"I'm so glad you're feeling better, sister. Can I do anything for you or get you anything?" Betty's tone a sticky sweet and a phony smile plastered on her face.

"Everything okay, Grandma?" Sebastian inquired with a scowl.

"Yes, Bubba. I'm okay. Look, here comes your grandpa. Open the door for him, will you?" Avoiding what could have become a very difficult situation with Jim, Erin changed the subject of conversation quickly. One look at Sebastian's face and Jim instantly knew something was not quite right.

"What's going on, Erin?" Jim asked. "Are you okay?"

"Yes, Jim, I'm good. Betty just stopped by to

say hello. You came in just in time to say goodbye to her. She was just leaving."

"Oh, nice. Say hi to Mike for me, Betty." And he walked out of the room with the pretext of having to wash his hands. He felt that Lady Luck was with him since he didn't have to spend any time with the family witch.

Another confrontation was over and, although it left a bad taste in Erin's mouth, she was happy to have learned more about her past. The best part was the fact that she was now definitely convinced that what she perceived as a dream, was, in fact, another memory. She could now see a small part of the picture. The puzzle was coming together.

"She's not all bad," Jim said, trying to convince Erin and perhaps even himself. He wiped his hands on the paper towel and sat on the sofa next to her.

"It's just that she's always been spoiled by everyone in the family. Including you. Whatever she wanted, she got. The main thing she wanted was attention. She thrives on it. Now, you don't remember her, her family, or your relationship with them. And, you're getting all of what she craves. You've got the whole family, friends, and acquaintances, doctors and hospital workers fussing all over you. You died and came back! You lost your memory, but she lost her place in all of this. Do you understand?"

"Is that what this is all about?" Erin's disbelief, evident in her pensive facial expression.

"She's jealous of my predicament? And, because of that, she treats Elaine badly? I don't care how she acts with me. By the way, she accuses me of pretending all of this. I can deal with that. But, I will not stay quiet when she disrespects Elaine."

"Oh, that," Jim replied. "She just thinks that since Elaine is the oldest niece, she should wait on her and her family when they come and visit. You know, out of respect, or so she says." He continued when he saw Erin's disgusted face. "Oh, yeah, Betty considers herself an 'elder' and demands that the younger generation, in this case Elaine, should wait on her. Now, that doesn't apply to her girls. They are exempt for some reason and don't have to lift a finger to wait on the other 'elders'. Oh, I remember: they are guests when they visit!"

"Okay, then," sassed Erin. "May I change how things transpire around here. Or, would I be crossing the family code?"

"No, by all means, cross her. Please!" Jim pleaded. "This is your home, and she is your sister. I know she acts like her life is perfect, but she's hasn't always had it easy. Grant you, at times her life decisions haven't been exactly the right ones and, like anyone else, she's had to suffer the consequences. Her married life hasn't been easy, either. Oh, she has plenty of money, and Mike gives her anything she wants, but he treats her like she doesn't have a brain and her opinion doesn't matter. Her job, according to Mike, is looking pretty and keeping their home like something out of a magazine. She makes up for it by acting like she knows everything and what's best for everyone else in addition to herself. Her thoughts are the most important. As you can see, her opinion of herself is quite high. She truly believes her way is the only way, especially when it comes to you.

"Like I said, she's not all bad. She just has some very old, bad habits and no one has ever called her on them. I think, with some finesse and a little firmness, you just might be able to change the way she sees things. It won't be easy: she's never been challenged and you, especially, have always given in to her. You've always been close, so she's not going to cut you out of her life. Nobody else wants to put up with her selfish attitude and she knows it.

"Oh, another thing: if you think she's hard to get along with, wait until you meet Mike, her husband. I'm sorry to say, he is really an annoying person.

"I've never had a problem with him, but you and him never got along. His opinion of the world is a bit warped. In his eyes, women know nothing and should stick to running a house and keeping their husbands happy. That's one of the reasons why you two always bumped heads. He's a pretty educated guy and he believes his opinion is the only one that counts. Nothing else matters, and no one is as important or knowledgeable as he is. By the way, he's a scientist. He says he's a rocket scientist, but who knows? I just know he has quite a few doctorates. He's a physicist and a chemist and who knows what else. One thing, though, he's not stupid. He won't go up against another male. Only the women. Especially one who contradicts him."

Maybe that was the queasy feeling that engulfed Erin when she saw his and Betty's wedding picture. Why were they so arrogant? Had life treated them so badly that making other people miserable was the only way for them to feel good about themselves?

Erin didn't like the feeling of conflict. She was having enough problems just getting to know everyone in her life. She didn't remember anything about these people, but what she did know was that no one had the right to make another person feel bad. It just wasn't proper.

There was another side to this that settled in her chest like a knife being twisted. Her only sister was treating her and her daughter so badly. Why did she attack Erin's situation and constantly belittle and call her a liar? Was that Erin's character before all this happened?

"Did I treat Betty badly?" Her thoughts plaguing her heart. "Did I ever lie to her? Did I cheat her in some way? Is this what a sister's relationship is like?" Erin's melancholy thoughts didn't last long.

"Grandpa," Sebastian interrupted. "Aunt Betty was being really mean and rude to Grandma. When she saw I was in the room, she started being... well... kinda like sticky syrup. You know, she didn't want anyone else to know she had been acting like a... you know, a witch."

"That's enough, Bubba," Erin scolded. "She's still your aunt and deserves a little respect. Well... maybe she doesn't deserve it, but she is still your elder. Understand?"

"Okay, Grandma." Sebastian wasn't happy that he wasn't allowed to finish tattling on his aunt, but he didn't argue. "I'll be in my room, doing homework." He walked towards the hallway and suddenly turned back quickly and said, "But it isn't right how she talks to you, Grandma." He swiftly escaped into his room and quietly closed the door.

Erin smiled and shook her head, then sighed deeply and exhaled with force, trying to understand her sister's attitude toward her. There was an apparent anger and hatred when she spoke with Erin and a condescending, demanding attitude toward Elaine. Even young Sebastian felt the animosity.

"Whew! I've learned a lot today. I'll work on Betty. Hopefully, we can come to some sort of civil tolerance of each other. But, there is no reason, and she has no right to treat Elaine with disrespect. I can't stomach that kind of attitude. And, I certainly don't want Sebastian confused by all this. Okay, enough of that. It's going to take time to iron that situation out. Right now, I have questions about us and our past together. Do you have some time?"

"Always, for you. What's up?" Jim sat alongside Erin on the couch, enjoying the closeness. Erin began by rehashing her memory of the family and the information that Betty had divulged.

Jim confirmed all the particulars, the sweet

along with the painful facts regarding Erin's family.

"They all meant well," he claimed. "They all were worried about your welfare. They just went about it all wrong. Your Uncle Max loved you like his own daughter and just wanted the best for you. But, you've gotta understand, it was wartime. He had experienced some of the worst of war, and he wanted to protect you from any possible hurt."

"So... did you meet me in Germany or who did?" Erin asked. Jim was already shaking his head before she finished.

"I had orders to go to Germany, so I left on that Monday after we returned from Ft. Worth. My brother's wife at the time, her name was Anna, had gotten you a ticket through her German-American Club to leave that Tuesday. Her friends were supposed to meet you at the airport in Frankfurt. But, it didn't happen that way. We never figured out what happened, but her friends never showed up. I got stuck in Ft. Dix, New Jersey. Consequently, you landed in Germany before I did, and no one was there to help you.

"So, being the independent woman that you are, you bought yourself a German-English dictionary when you got to Frankfurt Airport, changed some dollars to German marks and proceeded to the train station. You got a room at the Excelsior Hotel across the street from it until the next morning. You promptly sent your luggage ahead and found your way to Anna's mother's house in Fechenbach, in the south of Germany, and waited there until you heard from me. By the way, my sister-in-law's German, in case you hadn't figured that out already. It was her advice that helped you navigate through her country.

"When I finally got to Germany, my unit was sent out on maneuvers for six weeks. So, you stayed with her mom, Frau Fitzpatrick, until I could send for you. I wrote to you and explained the situation and, when you asked the old woman about staying in a guesthouse for the duration, she wouldn't hear of it. As it turned out, she was seventy-five and needed help preparing her house for winter.

"So, you made an arrangement. You scrubbed floors, cleaned windows, dusted, and cleaned for your room and paid for your food. It helped you out and helped her out as well."

"Frau Fitzpatrick had visited her daughter and my brother here in the States, so she knew me. He and I worked together and car-pooled to work, so the old Frau saw me almost every day for six months. Once you explained you were my wife, she opened her home and her heart."

"She spoke English?" Erin inquired.

"No," Jim answered. "But, the English/German dictionary you purchased at the airport proved to be invaluable to you and to her. In six weeks' time, that little book and the old woman taught you how to read, write, and speak German like a native. She took you around and introduced you to all the villagers, and they all took you under their wings and helped out with the lessons. Everyone got involved, from the two-year-old to the ninety-two-year old, and in that short period of time, they transformed you from young American woman to a proper, German Frau. You even dressed like a German lady. By the time we met up, you were fluent in the language and quite familiar with the culture and the German way of doing things. That knowledge and all you learned while living with the people sure made our life a heck of a lot easier later.

"I almost didn't recognize you when I picked you up at the train station. From the Fedora with the little feather in the hatband to the German shoes on your feet, you were decked out exactly like a German lady. Then you'd open your mouth and perfect German came out. The change was amazing, and I was impressed. Our time in Europe was an unbelievable and incredibly happy time in our lives."

"That's the memory I had when you brought me here to this house. I remembered the road to Fechenbach, riding along a river," Erin told Jim about her frightening thoughts that day, "I was afraid of getting into the train master's car. He kept saying 'Frau Fitzpatrick' and pointing to his Mercedes. I remembered looking at the river and thinking, 'Strange country, no one knows I'm here and he wants to take me somewhere'. I knew I didn't have a choice. This was my adventure, so I made the sign of the cross, prayed to whomever was listening, and got in the car."

"Fechenbach is on the River Main," Jim explained. "It took a whole lot of courage to go to a foreign country, not knowing anyone. My sister-in-law's mother knew you might seek her out, because she had received a letter from her daughter telling her you were traveling to Germany to meet up with me."

Another piece of the puzzle came together in Erin's mind and settled deep in her heart. She sat in the old recliner, once more staring out at the swaying palm trees. The gentle swishing of the palm fronds waving in the breeze brought a brief feeling of tranquility.

How is it that I'm surrounded by so much love and attention and yet I feel so alone? Frustrated, Erin pondered her emptiness. *I see my pictures everywhere and I know in my head, this is my life. Jim knows everything about me and my life with him, but, in my heart there's a strange chill. I want to love them all and believe who he says I am, but I don't know how.*

They do so much for me, and I sit here doing nothing and feeling sorry for myself. As Betty says, I allow them to wait on me as if I was the queen, giving nothing in return. And, all they want is for me to be happy and give them a small amount of love. Will I ever feel that I belong here?

She fixed her gaze on the trees moving rhythmically against the distant sky and the clouds above and behind, gently drifting by, aching for the memories to invade her thoughts and swallow her heart.

"I can't find the mustard!" shouted Bubba.

"It's in the fridge on the door shelf, sweetie," Erin answered. She sat up tall in the over-stuffed chair, astonished that she knew exactly where the yellow condiment was kept. She hadn't been in the kitchen for the longest time. She didn't remember where anything was kept, but, in that exact moment, she knew exactly the whereabouts of the mustard.

"Got it! Thanks, Grandma!" Bubba walked to the door and stared at Erin. His eyes wide with surprise.

"How did you know? Did you remember?"

"Yes," she answered, completely bewildered. They looked at each other, and their smiles turned into giggles. Another memory that made perfect sense and Erin was fired up, excited to be making progress.

A Heartache

The nightly routine was that, once the evening was through, Jim and Erin would go into their bedroom and Jim, or at times Elaine, would change Erin's bandages and tuck her into bed.

Jim would take his shower, and by the time he came out of the bathroom, Erin would pretend to be asleep. There were no good night kisses or caresses. Jim stayed on his side of the bed, and Erin pretended to snore quietly. But, on this particular night, Erin was waiting. She had questions that needed answers.

"Jim, don't you work?" she asked timidly.

"I did, we did," he replied. "We owned a small trucking company and had our own big rig. Believe it or not, at one time you, also had your commercial driving license and we team-drove together, cross country. We did that for about four years, then you started feeling sick, and it turned out you needed to have open heart surgery.

"Unfortunately, after the surgery, you didn't get to feeling any better. You were recuperating from the triple bypass well enough, but you were constantly complaining about back pain. You actually ended up in a wheelchair. You couldn't walk because the pain was so bad. It wasn't until recently that we found out that the lesion they found on your ovary back in March had grown tremendously and was putting pressure on your spine. That's what was causing all the pain. You had surgery to remove it and were doing great. It's when you came home that all of these crazy events began.

"It was one thing after another, so I decided that you needed me here at home more than we needed the truck. So, we sold the business. It's what you might call 'an early retirement'."

Erin didn't understand about retirement or about big rigs. What she did comprehend was that he sold their business to take care of her. Did he ask her opinion, or did he just decide this on his own? She didn't dare ask for fear of offending him. Whatever he did, he did it for her and that was all she needed to know.

"What about our son?" Erin's face was solemn. "You say he calls and asks about me. Does he not want to talk to me? What's up with him?"

"Yes, he calls often, he worries about you," Jim's smile dropped as he answered her question as delicately as he could. "But, he says there's no reason to speak with you, since you don't know who he is and certainly won't recognize his voice. Just another faceless person that you don't remember. He says he doesn't want to push you and add to your confusion.

"He's got his own way of thinking, and it's not always what we think is right. He'll come around. You'll see. Right now, don't worry about him. You've got enough on your plate." And, that was the end of that conversation.

Erin swallowed the information and didn't question it. But she was curious. Something in her heart ached, and she didn't understand the feeling.

Later, she thought, when he's ready.

Secret in the Closet

Erin leisurely strolled through the house, searching for anything that would spark a memory. There were drawers filled with papers that meant nothing to her. Birthday, Mother's Day, and an assortment of other holiday cards, written to her from various members of her family. Some she knew, others not. A blue box filled with old taxes, utility bills, odd and ends and random photos of people and places she didn't remember.

She wasn't searching for anything in particular, just looking, hoping that perhaps a note or a squiggle would jump out and make her feel something. Good or bad, she didn't care, just something that would trigger an emotion. She wanted her heart and soul to feel.

She decided her closet would be a good place to find interesting things. If nothing else, it could be fun.

Erin plopped on a large, platinum blonde wig on her head and glanced in the mirror. The giggles exploded from her chest. "Too funny! No, this is definitely not me!" she thought, but she didn't take it off. The hairpiece sat there hugging her head a bit lopsided as she continued to rummage thru old jewelry and ugly, much-too-small dresses.

Erin jumped, startled at the sound of Jim's voice. "Hey, what's going on here? Are you getting ready to go somewhere special? Or, are you planning to seduce me?" With his typical wink and a smile, he gave a hearty laugh.

"Nah, I'm just having some fun," Erin answered, pulling off the wig. They both started laughing and were so engrossed in the silliness that they didn't notice Betty standing in the doorway of the closet.

"I hope I'm not interrupting anything," her sarcastic tone putting a damper on their frivolity.

"No," said Jim, sarcastically. "Just some fun between a husband and wife." Tired of Betty's attitude and her inability or unwillingness to knock, Jim hoped she would back off and not antagonize Erin.

"What are you going to do with all this junk?" she inquired, her face distorted with disgust. She picked up a wig with her thumb and index finger, then quickly dropped it as if she was afraid it might bite her. "I don't understand why you don't get some hair implants instead of wearing these disgusting things." Betty's eyes scanned the shelves of the closet. Her face a picture of revulsion. "Good God, Erin. You still have clothes you wore in high school. Why do you hold on to this stuff? You know you're never going to fit in it anymore. You're at least a hundred pounds heavier, or more! Besides, it's all out of fashion. Just get rid of it!"

Elaine walked in just as Betty spit the nasty words out. "Why wasn't I invited to the party?"

"Oh, honey," answered Erin. "I was just having

some fun with your dad when Aunt Betty walked in. I guess I do need to thin out this closet."

"You ought to help your mother clean up this mess, Elaine" Betty ordered. "It's not healthy to have all this junk around, collecting dirt and spiders and who knows what else." At that precise moment, something vile crept up from Erin's stomach and landed in her mouth.

"Now, that's enough," she announced. "What makes you think it's okay to come in here, insult Elaine, and make me feel like a lazy idiot? You make fun of me with your sarcastic comments about how I look and how I don't clean or cook and how I treat Jim like a servant." Erin was on a roll and she couldn't stop her mouth from issuing everything she felt.

"Mom!" pleaded Elaine.

"No," said Erin. Her face sullen with hurt, her heart pounding against her chest and her entire body trembling. "I need to say this because this hostility needs to stop.

"Why, Betty? What gives you the right to always put us down? If you don't like it here, and it's obvious you can't stomach me or my daughter, then don't come over. I'm tired of hearing about how inept we are."

Shocked, Betty took a step towards Erin, her hands balled up into fists so tight, her neatly manicured nails dug into her palms. "How dare you talk to me like that? I'm your sister, the closest blood relative you have here. What's wrong with you? Did your brain snap when your heart stopped?"

"No, Betty," Erin whispered. "Just my ability to tolerate spoiled, snotty little sisters that have no manners and don't know when to keep their mouths shut."

Betty's face contorted and flushed with anger, her eyes like orbs of fire, shot death-looks to Erin.

"You, BITCH!," Betty growled. "You have the audacity to sit there and treat me like a nobody. After all I've done for you and Elaine. Talk about rights... I have every right! What you did to me was the most hurtful, damaging thing anyone could do to a woman, especially me, your sister. And, don't act like you don't remember. How convenient! She doesn't remember anything she doesn't want to remember."

"Betty," Jim interrupted. "Don't! This is not the time for this! Please!"

"Then when is the right time?" Betty retorted. "Her game is up! She can't remember? Well, let me enlighten her."

"Betty!" Jim's thunderous voice echoed in the small closet. Please, don't. Dr. Cabral says..."

"I don't give a damn what anyone says," Betty screeched, turning to Erin. "Just maybe it's what you need, dear sister. Something to shock you into recollecting your life and mine!"

"What is it? What are you shouting about?" Erin's words were perplexed, frightened. What was it she needed to know? This wasn't just a spoiled little sister wanting her way. This was the drama of a vengeful, angry woman, and all the hatred was directed at Erin.

"Somebody answer me!" Erin pleaded. Her eyes overflowing with tears. Without knowing why, she already knew that whatever it was, it was going to do damage. Damage to Elaine and to herself. She took a deep breath, wishing she could spare Elaine whatever evil was about to attack. But, she knew there was nothing she could do to prevent it.

With pleading in her eyes, she implored Jim. "You know what this is about?"

Jim's eyes told a sad story, but his lips didn't have a chance to say anything. Betty was ready to pounce on Erin.

"Oh, he knows, I'll have the privilege of telling you the truth of what you already know and are pretending to have forgotten. Yeah, right!

"You, who has the hard-working husband and the smart son and the beautiful daughter, a great life and so many friends. Yeah, the perfect life, everybody doting on you like you're the queen. Well, I'm about to snatch it away from you."

Elaine, gingerly attempting to tip-toe out of the room, jumped three feet backward when Betty grabbed her arm. "Stay put, Missy. This involves you, so you might as well snatch a seat and enjoy the fireworks."

Erin reached over and took Elaine's hand and squeezed. The mother's message loud, without words: "I'm here. Whatever it is, I'm here."

"Approximately twenty-one years ago, when you and Jim and Stephen were living in Germany," Betty started. "A fifteen-year-old girl came across the

Atlantic Ocean to visit you. But, she wasn't alone. She was carrying a child. She was five months pregnant, unwed and terrified. ME! I was making everyone around me crazy, including myself. Mom and Dad just thought I was lonely for you, so they sent me on a vacation.

"I needed help, I didn't know what to do. I didn't want anyone to know, and it was too late to do anything drastic, like get rid of it. So, I depended on your guidance, and you took advantage of my lack of experience."

"Wait just a minute," Jim interrupted. "It wasn't..."

"I'm telling this story," Betty broke in. Her fiery gaze planted directly at Erin. "You thought up a plan where you would pretend to be pregnant again and, when I had the baby, you would say it was yours. You'd explain that the baby came a little early and was born at home. It would be covered through the Military and would have the right to become a United States Citizen through Jim.

"No one would give me dirty looks, 'cause no one would be the wiser. I was naive, so I thought it was brilliant. You started wearing baggy clothes, just like me. But, I didn't go anywhere. I stayed in the house the whole time. For four months, I stayed hidden, like an unwanted animal.

"You told Mom and Dad, and all the folks back home, that you would home-school me in Europe, so I would get a broader education. And, they bought it. Everybody did.

"The big day arrived, and I went into labor. 'No problem', you said. 'I've taught Lamaze classes and delivered plenty of babies. I'll coach you through it'.

"And, so you did. We panted together and breathed as one. When it was time to push, we both pushed. After eighteen hours of crying and screaming and incredible pain, I, yes, I not you, gave birth to a beautiful baby girl.

"The rest was easy. Since you had already had a baby in Germany, it was just a matter of a sea of paperwork. Military forms and such and that was that. I pretended to be you and was admitted to the hospital. They examined me and the baby and released us. Another baby born abroad of American parents in the military. And, that was that."

Betty turned and faced a pallid, broken-down Elaine. "That's right, Missy. I'm your real mother. They've been hiding that fact from you, all your life. Stephen is your cousin, not your brother. And, this man," pointing at Jim, "is just an uncle."

Betty turned to Erin, "Now, tell me you don't remember doing all that, and I'll call you a damn liar."

No one spoke. The thick air choked with anger, mistrust, hate and even pity. Each sentiment had more than one owner. The one common denominator, pain! Each face grimaced with agony and lament for each other. Each pair of eyes, drowning in tears of sorrow.

All but one, Betty. Satisfaction encompassed not only her face but her whole body. She trembled with elation, her laughter euphoric at inflicting so much pain towards Erin. She never considered the anguish she was causing Elaine.

"I believe you've left out one, small detail," whispered Jim. His face long and distraught. "It was you who didn't want anyone to know you were with child. Your reputation as a 'good little fifteen-year-old girl' was ruined. Your life was over.

"You begged Erin to take the baby as her own. We both tried to talk you out of it, but your mind was made up and you had it all figured out. You would continue being the favorite daughter and the perfect, doting aunt. You would still be a free fifteen-year-old. Nothing would change as far as your life was concerned. No one would ever figure it out. In your eyes, everything would be perfect. It was you who planned every single detail, not Erin.

"You cried, you pleaded, you threatened to kill yourself if Erin didn't agree to do it. And, finally, against all that Erin believed in, Betty, and the love she had for you, she agreed to save your reputation and your life.

"And you're right, biologically we are not Elaine's parents. But, here, in our hearts where it counts, we have and always will love her like our daughter. Nothing you can say or do will ever change that. That, you can never take away from us, Betty."

"Elaine, get your things," Betty ordered. "You're going home with me. Yeah, you get to live in my beautiful house on the hill with the swimming pool you like so much. You'll have everything you ever wanted, and they couldn't afford to give you."

Elaine never did let go of Erin's hand. She slipped off the chair and knelt at her feet. She turned and looked up at Betty.

"Thank you for your offer, AUNT Betty." Tears running down her cheeks, quivering words escaping her heart. "But, I'm not going anywhere. I belong here with my mom and dad. This is my home."

"But, didn't you hear what I just said?" Betty argued, shaking in disbelief. "I'm your mother. Your place is with me, not her."

"Nothing has changed," stated Elaine. "We are all still family. What difference does it make who gave birth to me? I am loved by all of you and that will go on forever because we are blood. Let's just go on from here and stop trying to hurt each other.

"Aunt Betty, I understand you were very young, and you had a problem that needed a solution. Back in those days, the stigma of a fifteen-year-old having a baby without a husband would have been disaster. The difficulties for you and for me, let alone Grandpa and Grandma, as well as the rest of the family would have been devastating. So, you figured a way out of your predicament. Mom gave you what you needed because she loved you. She took your problem and carried it with her for the last twenty-one years. She never complained, she only loved. Can't you do that now? Just love and be grateful that it all turned out so well." Elaine's long and somber face cradled her tears in the wells of her dimples, never giving in to anything but hope.

Betty's head dropped, and her body shook violently. Suddenly, the consequences of her actions fell on her like a ton of anvils, crushing her selfish attitude as well as her entire life.

"Are you going to tell Mike?" Betty asked. But, it was more of a plea. "And my girls? What will they say and what will they think of me? You can't tell them! I forbid it!"

Erin stood up from her chair. Quietly, gently she put her thoughts into words. "As Elaine said, nothing has changed here. This is your chaos. You need to deal with it. If and what you tell your family is your business. We will deal with the mess you created here, in our little family. You have hurt no one but yourself. Go home, little sister. Think of what you will do with your family and the rest of your life." Slowly, Erin walked into her bathroom and closed the door. A mournful weeping was heard from within.

That evening, when all was still, Erin and Jim had a forceful, heartfelt conversation. None of it was easy, but it needed to be done, for both their sake.

Erin cleared her throat, took a labored breath and looked Jim directly in his eyes. "There are a couple of things that are festering in my head and, if I don't get them taken care of, I'm going to explode.

"I know that everything you do for me is because you think I need protecting or sheltering and I appreciate your concern. But, you seem to take pleasure in thinking and speaking for me, even though it makes me feel bad. Every time you make a decision without consulting me, asking me how I feel about something, or answering for me without taking my feelings into account, I get so upset, I want to throw up. Instead, I say nothing because I don't want you to think I'm ungrateful.

"Well, the next time you feel the need to do that, please don't. Just keep it to yourself. It may not make you feel any better, but you have no idea how great it would make me feel.

"You always tell me what I should or shouldn't do or say. I may not remember my past, but I'm quite capable of sorting through my present situation and figuring out what I want or don't want. I've lost my memory, not my ability to think for myself.

"I don't want to go through whatever life I have left having someone doing my thinking for me. Please, I appreciate all you've done and continue doing for me. But, there are some things I can do for myself. It'll keep you from offending me and me from resenting you.

"As for what happened today, I guess you had your reasons for not telling me something so important. And, since the 'Swiss cheese' up in my brain can't figure it out, I guess it's okay. I just want to get Elaine through it, and I don't want it to affect Bubba."

"I thought it would be too much for you too soon," Jim explained. "Too much trauma, after all you'd been through. I would have eventually told you. When the time was right.

"As for the other, you know, me running all

over you, I don't mean to. I guess, I just don't know the boundaries yet. In the old days, you just went along with whatever I said. You never questioned anything. You were... well..."

"Submissive," Erin finished his statement, her left eyebrow high on her forehead, her mouth in an over-extended scowl.

"Well, yeah, kind of," Jim answered. "I guess that's changed, huh?" And, with a wink and a smile, he melted Erin's heart.

Erin smiled. It was done.

Elaine had the most level head of all the adults. Perhaps in her heart, she believed or wanted to believe that nothing had changed. Although her head told her that she should feel something more than sympathy for Betty, her heart told her that Erin and Jim were her parents and always would be.

She felt extremely sorry for Betty, for she really hadn't accomplished anything in her favor. Out of a dark corner in her soul, Elaine wondered if Betty even knew who fathered the child she brought into the world.

"Will I ever know who my biological father is?" Elaine pondered. "Is it even important? No, not today, not ever. I have what counts and that's all I need."

Erin didn't remember the ugliness of the past. Consequently, all the hurt her family was feeling didn't settle in her heart. She wanted them all to be happy again but couldn't find the words to make it happen.

Erin reached over and pulled Elaine close to her, hugging her tightly, something she hadn't done to anyone. She whispered softly in Elaine's ear, "I can't change the past or do anything to make that better. But, I'm here right now, and, for what it's worth, I can't see my future without you being my daughter. I really don't know what this thing called love is... but, if it's anything like what I'm feeling right now, I'm giving it all to you, and it's yours to keep, for as long as you want me to be your mother."

In that exact minute, a loving bond formed. Perhaps it had always been there. But, in that instant, Erin felt the intensity of a mother's heart aching with a love for a child so deeply that no one could ever separate them. It was all-consuming.

Erin's feelings for Jim intensified. She felt the pain in his heart, and the weight of the load he had been carrying for so many years. In his face, Erin saw the love of a father trying to shelter his daughter from the past and that of a husband protecting his wife. Jim continued being the head of the house. His job of keeping everyone smiling and safe was what he did best. He was determined to make sure Erin was comfortable with all that had transpired, and that Elaine and Bubba felt loved and secure.

The only one that Erin felt was miserable was Betty.

Betty didn't visit for a long time and, when she finally did, she knocked on the door and waited to be asked to come in. She never apologized for the chaos she caused. She couldn't. In her small mind, she hadn't done anything wrong. She was the victim and, as such, she decided that, for the moment, she wouldn't tell her husband or daughters anything unless it was absolutely and catastrophically necessary.

Several days later, Betty showed up at Erin's home. The devastating scene that occurred on her last visit still fresh on her mind. She sat across from Erin, fidgeting with her car keys in her hand. She didn't want to instigate anything with Erin. Still, Betty felt he had a right to be there, despite the anger she was harboring. She justified her visit by saying, "I'm on my way to the store, and I just wanted to know if you were okay or if you needed anything. Since it's obvious you're fine, I'll leave and let you get back to whatever it is you do."

Betty tucked away, in the secret compartment of her heart, the pain, the fear, and the regret of giving up her daughter so many years ago. Then, without a second thought, she stood tall, inhaled deeply and walked out the door.

Without weighing her words or caring who could hear them, she grumbled out loud, "It's Elaine's loss. With me, she could have money, clothes, a car and a fabulous home to live in. She could be free of that bratty, snotty boy of hers, too. He would stay right where he is. He wouldn't move into my house, that's for sure. But, no! Instead, Elaine chooses to live with Erin in that shabby, rundown two-bedroom rat's nest. Stuck raising a kid without a father. Too bad he died in the military or I would have sent the pip-squeak straight to him," Betty rambled on. Some of her thoughts were coherent. Others, scrambled and twisted. She wasn't ready to let things go. She couldn't. She didn't know how.

Much to Erin's surprise, her heart ached. For the first time, Erin felt the emptiness of a sister's hate, and it hurt deeply.

"I won't give up on you, despite your attitude, little sister. I'll be here when you're ready."

Accepting Destiny

That night, feeling the chill of the winter night, and the icy events of the afternoon, Erin lay in bed, curled up in a ball under a heavy blanket, shivering. If she wanted another blanket, she would need to wake Jim and that was something she absolutely did not want to do.

Every night when they were in bed together, Erin did her best to stay on her side of the bed, where there would be no physical contact. She refused to give Jim any false hopes or to do anything that might encourage him. In her mind, an intimate, romantic relationship was not what they had. Theirs was a comfortable, friendly understanding. And, that's how she thought she wanted it to remain.

Jim was snoring softly and sleeping so soundly, she didn't want to disturb him. But, she couldn't keep from shaking. Her feet felt like ice. She thought perhaps it was the trauma of the day that had her so cold. Or, maybe it was just the weather. Whatever it was, she was chilled, through and through.

Erin couldn't stand the bitter cold any longer and finally decided there was no other way. She reached out to touch Jim's arm and ask him to get her another blanket. When her fingertips got close to him, her chilled hand felt the warmth of his arm and immediately she yearned to grasp it.

After much, intense deliberation, she decided that if she inched closer to him, she might be able to warm her whole body without waking him.

Stealthily, she moved closer to Jim, and a delicious heat radiated from his body toward hers. Carefully, so as not to disrupt his sleep, Erin cautiously turned on her side, inching her backside as close as she could to Jim's body, without touching him. All she wanted was to get warm. Nothing else. The last thing on her mind was for him to wake up and catch her warming herself at his expense.

Just a little closer and I'll get warm, relax and fall asleep, Erin thought.

But, relaxing and falling asleep was not something Erin could control. She was getting warm, slowly. But, her frozen feet ached, her teeth chattered and her whole body still quivered. She still needed that blanket.

"Maybe if I just move my feet a little more toward his, I'll be okay," she contemplated. Slowly, holding her breath and keeping her eyes closed tight, she slid her right foot toward the warmth in the bed.

Jim stirred, and Erin froze. Not one cell in her body moved. Not one breath escaped her. Her head cautioned to forget the whole thing and just wake Jim and ask for the blanket. But, her body yearned to get closer and take advantage of the delightful heat his body was giving off, without his knowledge or help.

Quietly, she exhaled, savoring the luxurious comfort thawing her icy back and feet. Without thinking about it, without planning and completely out of her control, Erin sighed and allowed her body to relax and embrace the pleasure of Jim's unknowing and unwilling services. As her body accepted the cozy warmth, a soft wave of sleep overtook any objections she might have conjured up. Without planning it, Erin fell into a deep, comfortable slumber.

A soft whir in her ear interrupted Erin's thoroughly delicious sleeping, and a delicate breeze caressed the back of her neck and the side of her cheek, causing her to squint.

What is that? she thought, gingerly attempting to swat whatever was annoying her. As she raised her arm, alarmed, Erin realized that something was wrapped around her waist, and it wasn't the blanket.

Her eyes flew open and she took a sharp, deep breath. Jim's arm, firm and snug, was wrapped around her body, encasing her like a cocoon. He was totally unaware, sound asleep. Just as she had been.

"What do I do? This can't be." Erin's thoughts told her to make a fuss and get away from him. But, her body responded quite the opposite. She couldn't remember the last time she had felt so warm, comfortable and exquisitely wonderful. She knew she belonged exactly where she was, doing exactly what she was doing, enjoying every second of Jim's natural heat. Maybe, this was because he was asleep, and she could relish all these new feelings alone. Perhaps, it was because she felt like she belonged exactly where and how she was at that very moment. He wasn't in control, she was! It was her decision and hers alone to take pleasure in the moment or to change the situation. And, her decision had been made, without a conscious effort. Her body made it for her, and she loved it.

It didn't matter. At that precise moment, nothing mattered. Slowly, Erin lowered her arm and gently placed her hand on Jim's forearm. He stirred and inched closer to her, still deep in his slumber. Breathless, she savored the sultriness of his body against hers. The two main pieces of her scattered puzzle had come together and fit perfectly.

She didn't remember her past and could only see bits and pieces of their life together. But, she now knew she was ready to embrace her present and her future. She could make new memories with her family.

No longer would she feel sorry for herself for what she didn't remember, what was lost and was gone. Whether or not she regained some or all of her past wasn't important. What did matter was the current opportunity to love and be loved by this man and the family surrounding her.

Erin had been given so many gifts. First and foremost, her life encompassed so many blessings. She could wake up every morning and get out of bed. She could walk and communicate without difficulty. She could think and make decisions regarding her life. And, most importantly, she had so many who loved her in so many different ways and all ways were welcome.

Slowly, Erin exhaled, allowing her body to relax her muscles and her frightened inhibitions. Her eyes closed, and her mind drifted to a place filled with tranquility. Finally, she wasn't afraid of what might happen with this man next to her. His soft snore and his light embrace produced a much needed and much wanted peace. She drifted off warm and secure, feeling that all was as it should be.

The Nightmare

"NOOOOOOOOOOOO!" Erin screamed, her voice a thunderous lament. Her hands were balled up into two tight fists thrusting into the air, fighting an invisible attacker. Her knees and legs cycled up and down. She kicked, her body twisted and lifted up off the mattress and then fell back onto her spine. Spasms contorted every inch of her human form. Unintelligible words spewed from her mouth. Erin's eyes bulged one moment and then shut and squeezed tight the next. Her distorted face was streaked with tears

Jim's peaceful slumber abruptly ended, and fear exploded, not knowing how to protect his wife.

"Erin!" he yelled. "Erin, wake up. It's me, Jim. Honey, I'm right here. Baby, wake up, you're okay, you're just dreaming, wake up, Erin!"

But, Erin didn't hear Jim's agitated words. Her shouts echoed throughout the house. Jim feverishly attempted to keep Erin from falling off the bed and hurting herself. Her arms flailed wildly, as she fought the invisible assailant for her life.

Despite Jim's size in contrast to Erin's, subduing and calming his wife, at that moment, was one of the most difficult tasks he had ever encountered. He needed to use his strength, yet didn't want to force her into submission. His voice echoed firmly and lovingly at the same time. The struggle continued as the minutes seemed to fly by. Then, somehow, Jim's arms finally surrounded Erin. He tightened his embrace, constraining her movements, constantly speaking soft words to soothe Erin's nightmare and bring her out of her ferocious battle.

After much coaxing and gentle whispers, Erin's eyes suddenly focused. At that same moment, the bedroom door flew open and Elaine and Sebastian burst into the room. Alarmed beyond words, Elaine's tears flowed freely, as she held on tight to Sebastian.

"Is she alright, Dad?" Elaine pleaded.

"Yes," he answered. "Go back to bed, she's just had a nightmare. Everything's okay. Go back to bed." He looked up from the frozen position, his arms locked tight around Erin. "It's okay, Bubba. Grandma just had a bad dream. She's fine now. Go back to bed."

Elaine closed the door, and Erin's sobs seemed to quiet down.

"Oh my God, oh my God! It was a little girl. I saw a little girl, and she was holding her breath. She didn't want to breathe. Because... because... he was touching her. He had one hand over her mouth and the other hand... the other hand was touching her privates. He was trying to lick her body, and he was hurting her. He kept saying, "Shh, pretty baby. Shhhhh!" She was so scared, she couldn't move. The intense fear had her paralyzed. She was little, and he wouldn't stop! Oh... my... God!

"NOOOO! WAIT... it was a woman, then it was a man, again. I'm going crazy! GOD... I'm so confused. First, it was a little girl, then it was me, like I am now, and the man with the little girl turned into a woman. And... she was grabbing me, putting her fingers in my... OH MY GOD! Oh, Jim! What's wrong with me? What happened?"

The tears poured down her face, choking Erin, inhibiting her normal breathing. Her heart pounded in her chest, exploding the fear, anger and uncontrollable panic.

"It was a bad dream," Jim softly explained. "It's over. You're safe. The little girl is safe. No one is hurting her. It's just a bad dream. I'm right here and everything is okay. Breathe, Erin. Just breathe."

His embrace never relaxed. Jim patiently waited as Erin's tense body tried to let go of the terror.

"What was that, Jim?" Her voice quivered, her body still shook from the horrendous fright. Suddenly she screamed at him, her eyes wild with terror. "Let go of me!" she screeched. "Why are you hurting me?"

Jim let Erin go and pulled back, his heart breaking while he watched his wife's tortured facial expressions, her body language shouting defensively.

"Why did I see that? I can still see the little girl, but I don't know her. Did it really happen? What was that?"

"Easy, Erin," soothingly Jim suggested. "Relax, honey. It was just a nightmare."

"No, Jim!" Erin looked up at him. "Tell me the truth! Something so awful, so hateful, so incredibly wrong, had to be real. Look at me Jim, that was a memory, wasn't it? Don't hide this from me. I need to know the truth. What was that? Who was the little girl? Who was that monster who was touching her? And, the woman, touching me, who was that and why do I feel so violated and dirty? Quit telling me it was just a dream. Something that real and that terrifying can't be just a dream. TELL ME! Please! I need to help her. I need to do something to save her. Help me, Jim. Please!"

Jim reached out and Erin wailed, "Don't touch me!"

Immediately he moved back, his hands up and open in front of him. "Okay, easy, Erin. No one is hurting anyone! And, the little girl is okay. Yes, honey, is was a memory. A very bad, ugly and hurtful memory. In fact, it was several memories, all mixed up into one. But, it's over. It happened a long time ago, and it's all over."

"Tell me, Jim." Erin's voice low, calm and a sickened look on her face told Jim she needed to know every sordid detail.

"Again, it was a very long time ago, and the most important thing you need to know is that the little girl is safe. The culprit who attacked her is dead, so he can't hurt anyone, anymore."

"Who was the little girl?" Erin's words came out loud and demanding. "Is she alive, did she survive this horror? Where is she, who is she? Tell me, Jim, was it Elaine?"

"No, Erin," he replied. "What you described wasn't Elaine. And, everything is fine now. Please, Erin. Try and calm down."

Erin took a deep breath, her facial expression suddenly changed. No longer was her body language displaying angst or frustration, but a strong determination.

"It doesn't matter? Whomever she is, doesn't matter, does it?"

Erin stared at Jim, resigned, beaten. "Tonight, I saw a little girl, frightened and being abused and physically hurt. But, I don't know her. I don't know anyone. How is it that I can remember something so horrific, but I can't remember the child, or the man that abused her? How stupid am I that I can't help her? You say he's dead. Did they get him before he hurt anyone else?" Erin had many questions. She knew Jim had the answers, and she wasn't ready to wait for another day to know the truth.

"Yes, Erin," Jim answered. "He was caught and sent to prison and, after many years, that's where he died."

"Who was he?" Erin asked.

"He was an old friend of the family," Jim replied. "As a matter of fact, he was Betty's godfather. But, that's not important, honey. It's over."

"And, the little girl, who is she and why did I experience this nightmare?"

"You, Erin. You are the little girl that you saw in your dream." Jim's face was desolate, his heart wishing he could eliminate all the pain that engulfed the woman that he loved. "He did try to harm Elaine and, it just so happens, you walked in on him - just in time, I might add. He didn't do anything to Elaine, thanks to you and your ever-vigilant mother's heart. Naturally, we pressed charges and, when you described what he did to you and Betty when you were little girls, others came forward to also accused him. He was convicted and sent to the state penitentiary.

"Betty said he never touched her, and she never forgave you for, as she put it, causing him so much trouble. He was her godfather, and she said she loved him. And, she was sure he loved her. Probably because he was always buying her things and giving her money. You know your sister.

"Either way, it was your courage that saved Elaine and so many other little girls. And, who knows, maybe little boys, too.

"Anyway, it's over, he's dead."

"What about the woman I saw?" Erin wasn't asking anymore. She was pleading for answers. "I know you can't climb into my head and know exactly who I saw. But, do you have any idea what I'm talking about?"

"Yes, Erin. That also happened. Remember I told you that you were very ill and had surgery to remove your breasts? Well, that's when a hospital employee sexually assaulted you. The woman in your nightmare was a nurse. A very sick individual. The law took care of her, too. I'm so sorry that, of all things to surface in your memory, it had to be those. But, I guess, along with the good memories, some of the bad will also come back to you. It's part of life, and it can't be avoided."

Erin fell silent. Her tears had dried, and her shaking had subsided. But, the tight knot in her throat persisted. She longed for memories that would comfort her and perhaps even make her laugh. Happy thoughts to make her feel some the good that was part of her prior life.

She looked up and saw all the hurt in Jim's face. He had shouldered so many ugly moments because of her. Yet, here he was, at her side, trying to protect her and help her through every single miserable torment. He didn't complain or judge. Patience and love were the only emotions he allowed to come through.

Erin reached out and took his hand, and much to Jim's surprise and her's, she kissed his palm tenderly. She had no idea why and without overthinking it, she instinctively followed her heart. Was this love? Maybe, she didn't know. What she did understand was that on this day, at this moment, she didn't want to be with anyone else.

She needed his strength to help nurture hers. How many more ugly things would shroud her? She knew Jim was right: the good with the bad happens in life, and Erin didn't have control over any of it.

"Does everyone know about the things that happened to me as a little girl?" Erin asked Jim.

"No, not everyone," He answered. "It's

nobody's business, so don't worry about it. As for what happened to you in the hospital, much of our family knows, but not to what extent. You know, not the particulars. Please, Erin. Don't dwell on it. It's over, honey. Let it go." Jim placed his arm around Erin's shoulders. And, once again, she pulled away. Her face fell, long and pensive and her eyebrows furrowed together. She stood and walked toward the window seat.

Suddenly, her eyes shut tight and the tortured look on her contorted face demonstrated a pain deep in her soul.

Their mama had gone to the corner grocery store to pick up some milk and bologna. She promised to be back in about twenty minutes.

He must have been watching from the corner, because as soon as Mama left, Erin heard his car turn the corner towards the house. She knew that sound all too well and immediately jumped into action.

"Hurry, Betty, we have to hide." Fast as their small feet could carry them, Erin pulled Betty through the kitchen door, slamming it shut behind them. They slipped into the laundry room, closing that door as well.

"Shhh, don't breathe, Betty," Erin's said, her voice below even a whisper. She and Betty were in the corner between the washer and the dryer, right behind the door, crouched underneath a pile of dirty clothes and an old bedspread.

"We're playing the hiding game again, Betty.

So, we're gonna pretend that nobody is home. We have to fool him to think we went shopping with Mama, so he'll go away. And, we have to act like we can't talk. We can't even breathe, 'cause he'll hear us. Okay?" Betty didn't answer, she just nodded her head with extreme urgency.

The two little girls heard the car's engine turn off, and the car door open and slam shut. Heavy footsteps resounded on the tile kitchen floor and, when the back door creaked open, his thick, raspy voice was heard, just above a whisper.

"Come out, come out, wherever you are, girls. I know you're here." What should have sounded like a silly sing-song melody was heard by the terror-stricken sisters as a warning to shrink their bodies so small, that not even their heartbeats could be felt, for fear of alerting the intruder to their whereabouts.

Betty softly whimpered and Erin, slower than the movement of a snail, reached up and quickly slid her hand over Betty's mouth. "Shhh, don't breathe, Betty!"

He kept calling to them, swiftly moving from room to room, looking under the beds, in the closets, and in the cupboards under the sink.

Finally, he stood at the open kitchen door again and angrily, he murmured, "I guess they went with their mom."

He closed the door and, as quickly as he had gone into the house, he ran out the front door and got into his car.

The girls never moved.

"Shhhhh! Not yet, Betty. The game's not over until his car gets to the corner and we can't hear it anymore."

The tires screeched as he took the corner at high speed, and immediately the little ones clawed their way out from under the pile of dirty tee shirts and underwear, their faces a blotchy red from lack of air and their necks and backs dampened with nervous sweat.

"Yuck!" shouted Betty. "Did we win?"

"Yes," answered Erin. "This time, we won."

From deep in her body, a loud, heavy growl escaped Erin's lips. Tears welled up and poured down her face. Her dismal cries, like that of a wounded animal, rushed out of her chest and away from her soul.

This memory was raw and ripped through Erin's body and tore at her heart. The recollection of his hand slithering down her body and his hot, nasty breath on her chest, breasts, and private areas turned her stomach upside down and filled her mouth and throat with bile, gagging her. She shivered as her shoulders hunched and her legs gave way.

Jim quickly moved towards Erin and embraced her, breaking her fall to the ground. This time she didn't flinch. She lay her head on his chest, allowing her shaking body to lean against his. Then, she sobbed violently, vomiting up the bile of emotions, pain, and anguish until there was nothing left.

"No one will ever hurt you again," Jim whispered. "I promise." Erin looked up at Jim, her eyes full of questions that she didn't want answered.

"You know about all of this," Erin asked. "Does Betty remember?"

"I know what you've told me. The details you've kept to yourself. As for Betty, you and she have had some talks about it. When he died, she denied most of it. She said he had tried to molest her, but nothing really happened. Then, she acted like a little girl on her birthday. She celebrated, laughing and singing. Nothing was ever brought up again. She refused to talk about it and said you were crazy.

"On that day, you looked relieved, Erin. You said you felt sorry for the horrible life he had led and were grateful, knowing he would never hurt anyone else again."

Life Continues

Erin continued to have snippets of memories, some longer and more detailed than others. Some happy, others painful. It was a mixture of life events. Most didn't make sense because she couldn't remember the people involved. But, little by little, day by day. With the help of her family, her friends, and Dr. Cabral, Erin became, if not comfortable, more tolerant of her situation.

The relationship with Jim changed for the better. The friendship grew, and her dependence on him became more relaxed. Not for what he could do for her, to help her regain her life back, but for the love and tenderness that he gave her whenever she needed or wanted it.

In time, she learned that he too, depended on her. For her friendship, her wit, and her sense of compassion. Intimacy took time to develop and, although it wasn't easy, Erin began to look forward to Jim's presence and, even more than that, his effortless way of making her smile. And, on one, cozy Saturday afternoon, while Elaine and Sebastian were at the movies, Jim's natural heat gently thawed Erin's fears and inhibitions. She allowed him to teach her what love was.

"Making love is not just the physical," Jim explained. "But, the act of pleasing the person you're with to the best of your ability, here, in your heart.

Making that person happy, above all else. And, that's what I wish for you: happiness. Whatever was in the past (good or bad), is in the past. I want to give and show you happiness and fulfillment, now. They say that tomorrow isn't promised to anyone. You and I, more than anyone, know that to be a fact. So, we need to enjoy the present to the fullest.

"That's what I believe and what you used to believe love is, caring for each other. Being there when times are easy and supporting each other when times are hard. The physical pleasure is an added bonus." As always, Jim's smile and his actions proved what his heart felt and so much more than his words expressed.

Epilogue

Erin's abdominal wound took about eight months to heal completely. Her psychological trauma, to this day, still causes uncertainties. She continues to struggle with her memories or lack of, and she refers to this issue as "Swiss cheese". Some things she remembers with accuracy and vivid detail. Others, (the holes in the cheese), remain a mystery and totally evade her memory.

Erin has still not found herself, but she continues her search. In her heart, she knows that every day gives her new possibilities, and every day she discovers more about herself and her family grateful for the opportunity to love and be loved.

Jim devotes his life to Erin's happiness and well-being. He gives her the space she desires but is there if she needs or wants his assistance. Each day together is an adventure, full of surprises, love, and laughter. It's what he lives for, to please and love his Erin.

Erin's son, Stephen got a transfer and moved back to California. After all that his mother had gone through, he thought it best to be near her, whether she recognized him or not. She still has no recollection of him. But, they have become close, and their relationship is flourishing.

Elaine has found a love in her life. She and Sebastian will be moving to their own house, not too far away, after her marriage. She stays close to her mother and helps Jim whenever necessary. She and Erin have become best friends.

Sebastian is developing into a handsome teenager that adores his grandmother. He spends much of his leisure time, working and/or playing on computers, sure in the knowledge that if he continues to study, he will change world technology, one computer and one application at a time.

Betty learned a few lessons about how life truly is. Her attitude has not changed completely. But, to stay close to her sister, she thinks before she speaks. She still doesn't always hold her tongue, but she knows better than to antagonize Erin. Her relationship with Elaine continues to be strained. Elaine calls it a 'work in progress'.

The friendship with Dr. Cabral continues to grow and has blossomed into a beautiful relationship, not only with the doctor, but with her family as well.

Erin maintains the feeling that she will never be able to repay Dr. Cabral for saving her life, for how does one put a price on something so precious? It's impossible. Sending her an abundance of love, hugs, and grateful sentiments can never be enough. Yet, Erin remains diligent in her efforts to show her gratitude and immense affection for the beautiful young doctor who brought her back from the other side of life.

Glossary

Am-Bu Bag - A hand held device commonly used to provide positive pressure ventilation to patients who are not breathing or not breathing adequately.

CPR – Cardio Pulmonary Resuscitation

Intubation – A tube inserted into the larynx (voice box)

Cardiac Board- A hard board placed under the patient's upper body for resuscitation purposes

Crash Cart – A supply cart used for emergency resuscitation

I.V.- Intravenous
E.R. - Emergency Room
I.C.U. - Intensive Care Unit
C.C.U. - Cardiac Care Unit
Defibrillator – a machine used to arrest the fibrillation of (heart muscle) by applying electric shock across the chest, thus depolarizing the heart cells and allowing normal rhythm to return.

Author's Note

Although the contents of this endeavor were created, exploited, and manipulated in my head and my heart, 'Finding Erin' is fictional, inspired by actual events. I have drawn on these incidents to tell a story about a woman whose heart stops for an undetermined amount of time, consequently losing both her short-term and long-term, memory. This is not unlike what occurred to me, your humble writer.

In real life, I continue to work through my challenges with memory loss and, to this day, eleven years later, there are some concepts that I recall in minute detail, while other elements of my life slip through and remain lost in a deep, bottomless hole. This is what I refer to as 'Swiss cheese' in my brain.

I have recovered much of my long term-memory and, for that, I am immensely grateful. But, there are still many recollections of simple thoughts and images that elude me.

As for my short-term memory, there are days that I repeat myself, sometimes once or twice and other times more than that. However, friends and family, familiar with the situation, continue to indulge me with patience, encouragement, and many, many smiles. All are delighted and thankful just to be together and to continue to have me alive and still in their midst. Me being the most appreciative of all.

My family and close friends, and many

acquaintances are a daily reminder that memories, as well as life itself, are precious and should not be taken for granted. What we have today, in real life or in our thoughts, can be lost in a heartbeat.

The character of Dr. Sara Cabral is, in fact, Dr. Sonia Ceballos, an actual physician and surgeon, who continues attending to and caring for as many patients as she possibly can see in a day. She has a thriving practice and saving lives is what she expertly does with her skills and her heart. She works more hours than there are in a day and more days than can be counted on a calendar, loving every moment of her exhilarating, busy life.

The strong, intense bond that formed between a simple patient and a young intern, so many years ago, has matured and intensified over the years and continues to flourish. Now, to include not only Dr. Ceballos and myself but our loving families as well.

My husband voices to all who will listen that Dr. Ceballos not only saved my life but his as well. He feels that he owes more than he can ever repay the young physician in several lifetimes.

All other characters and situations are creations of my vivid and colorful imagination. My goal was to entertain the reader while giving a little insight as to the challenges of memory loss, both from the patient's view as well as that of the family, friends, and acquaintances that must cope with this type of difficult and, at times, extremely challenging condition.

www.ingramcontent.com/pod-product-compliance
Lightning Source LLC
Chambersburg PA
CBHW050931120626
46552CB00001B/157